Thomas William Allies

The see of St. Peter, the rock of the church, the source of

jurisdiction, and the centre of unity

Fourth Edition

Thomas William Allies

The see of St. Peter, the rock of the church, the source of jurisdiction, and the centre of unity
Fourth Edition

ISBN/EAN: 9783337261702

Printed in Europe, USA, Canada, Australia, Japan

Cover: Foto ©Andreas Hilbeck / pixelio.de

More available books at **www.hansebooks.com**

THE SEE OF S. PETER

THE

SEE OF S. PETER

THE ROCK OF THE CHURCH

THE SOURCE OF JURISDICTION

AND

THE CENTRE OF UNITY

BY

THOMAS WILLIAM ALLIES, K.C.S.G.

FOURTH EDITION

Numerate Sacerdotes vel ab ipsa Petri Sede,
Et in ordine illo patrum quis cui successit videte ;
Ipsa est PETRA, quam non vincunt superbæ inferorum portæ.
　　　　　　　S. Augst. *Psalm. cont. part Donati.*

LONDON

CATHOLIC TRUTH SOCIETY

21 WESTMINSTER BRIDGE ROAD, S.E.

1896

TO

POPE LEO XIII.

THIS LITTLE WORK, ONCE HONOURED

BY THE APPROVAL OF HIS PREDECESSOR PIUS IX.

AT ITS FIRST APPEARANCE IN 1850,

NOW REPUBLISHED AT HIS DESIRE,

IS MOST HUMBLY OFFERED

IN REVERENCE BY

THE AUTHOR.

PREFACE.

SOME years ago the writer, already in great distress of mind at the historical and actual position of the Anglican Church, at the statements of her formularies, at the want of shape and principle in her practice, and, above all, at her general character and temperament as a communion which seemed to him thoroughly alien from the spirit of the ancient Fathers, betook himself to the special consideration of one point,—the Primacy of the Roman See,—which he thought more calculated than any other to lead him to a sure conclusion. He was then, as he is now, "convinced that the whole question between the Roman Church and ourselves, as well as the Eastern Church, turns upon the Papal Supremacy, as at present claimed, being of divine right, or not. *If it be*, then have we nothing else to do but submit ourselves to the authority of Rome ; and better it were to do so before we meet the attack, which is close at hand, of an enemy who bears equal hatred to ourselves and Rome ;— the predicted Lawless One, the Logos, reason, or private judgment of apostate humanity rising up against the Divine Logos, incarnate in His Church."

The writer, moreover, then professed, that "he took up this inquiry for the purpose of satisfying his own mind;" that "had he found the Councils and Fathers of the Church, before the division of the East and West, bearing witness *to* the Roman Supremacy, as at present claimed, instead of *against* it, *he should have felt bound to obey them;*" and that "as a Priest of the Church Catholic in England he desires to hold, and to the best of his ability will teach, all doctrine which the undivided Church always held." [1]

He made these professions in the simplicity, it is true, but likewise in the sincerity of his heart; and he made them publicly before God and man. Now, the conclusion to which he was at that time led by the study of antiquity was, that a Primacy [2] of divine institution had indeed been given to the See of Peter, but that the degree to which it had been pressed in later times formed an excuse for those communions which, *while they maintained*

[1] *The Church of England cleared from the Charge of Schism,* Advertisement.

[2] This is admitted in p. 313, p. 315, and pp. 490, 491 of the second edition of the above-mentioned work. The author ought to have seen what it involved; for no *abuse,* even could such be proved to exist, would warrant men in rejecting what is of *divine* institution. This was once put to him in a very forcible way by a much-valued friend: "If God has instituted Baptism, men would not be justified in rejecting it, even if the Church were to administer it with spittle."

the Catholic faith whole and entire, were *de facto* severed from it.

Thus he made these professions when he thought that they led him to one conclusion ; but he is equally bound to redeem them now that in the course of years they have led him to another.

For though his study of the question terminated for the moment at this point, yet the Supremacy claimed by S. Peter's See over the whole Church was a subject never out of his thoughts. And in the meantime what he saw of the actual state of the Roman Communion in other lands, of the principles on which it was based, and of the fruits which it produced, deeply moved and affected him. That Communion seemed in full possession of the great sacerdotal and sacramental system for which earnest Anglicans were vainly struggling, as well as of that religious unity the name of which in an Anglican mouth sounded like a mockery, amid the deep contradictions, both as to principles and as to practice, which are equally tolerated and supported by the Establishment ; when just at this moment that one only doctrine of all those mooted at the Reformation, which had appeared to him to be as unquestionably taught, at least by the formularies of the Anglican Church, as by the ancient Church—the doctrine of Baptismal Regeneration—was brought before the tribunal of the Court of Arches, and thence carried, by appeal, to the Queen in Council.

This fact first brought home to the writer the real nature of the Royal Supremacy. Up to that time, without having accurately looked into that power, he had supposed it to be *practically* indeed a great tyranny over the Church subject to it, but *in principle* only "a supreme civil power over all persons and causes in temporal things, and over the temporal accidents of spiritual things."[1] But the more he considered it in its origin, and with reference to the power which it supplanted and succeeded, and in its exercise during three hundred years, and in its whole tone and demeanour to the communion over which it was "supreme governor," the more painfully he became convinced that such a limitation, desirable as it might be to quiet the consciences of churchmen, was *as a fact* quite untenable. He felt that at his Anglican ordination as Deacon and as Priest, and subsequently, he had taken an oath of obedience to a power the nature and bearing of which he did not then at all comprehend—a power which, the moment he came to comprehend it, seemed to be utterly opposed to every principle which he held dear as a Churchman, and to contradict as much the relation of the Church to the State which is set forth in the Holy Scriptures as the teaching of the Fathers and the acts of General Councils,—a power which had

[1] So stated in the circular put forth by Archdeacons Manning and Wilberforce, and Dr. Mill.

no parallel in all historical Christianity up to the
very time of its enactment, and which not merely
enthralled, but destroyed, the continuous life of
the Church. For he found that Supremacy of the
civil power to consist in a supreme jurisdiction
over the Establishment in matters both of faith and
of discipline, and in the derivation of Episcopal
mission and jurisdiction—not as to their *origin*
indeed, but as to their *exercise*—from the Crown or
the nation. The writer at once felt that he must
repudiate either that Supremacy or every notion of
the Church; that is, the one divinely-constituted
Society to which the possession of the truth is
guaranteed, and which has a continuous mission
from our Lord for the spiritual government of souls
and the building up that humanity which He re-
deemed " to the measure of the stature of the perfect man." The Royal Supremacy and the Church
of God are two ideas absolutely incompatible and
contradictory.

But my heart, my soul, my conscience, and no
less my reason, every power and principle within
me, were longing, sighing, thirsting for the Church
of God, " the pillar and the ground of the truth."

Any decision to which the Queen in Council
might come was unimportant in my sight, in com-
parison to the fact that the Queen in Council had
the power of deciding in matters of doctrine.

Thus I felt before the decision came out ; but

when it came out there was added a sense of shame, of degradation, and of infamy, which had never before oppressed me, in that I belonged to a communion of which the supreme tribunal, when called upon to declare whether, by its existing rule of doctrine, infants were or were not regenerated by God in holy Baptism, decided neither that they were nor that they were not, but that the Clergy might believe and teach either one or the other, or both indifferently.

And I felt thus because *any* error and *any* heresy are innocent and innocuous compared to the tenet that error and heresy are indifferent; and *any* legal decision, however erroneous, is *honourable* compared to that which pronounces it equally lawful to believe and teach that God the Holy Ghost is given, and that He is not given, to a child by a certain act.

Nor can I regard the institution of Mr. Gorham by the Court, and at the fiat of the Archbishop of Canterbury, under the decree of Her Majesty as Supreme Governor of the Anglican Church, to be anything else but a public profession that the Anglican Church is founded on the most dishonest compromise—one which involves the denial of the whole Christian faith and the practical establishment of unlimited Latitudinarianism.[1]

---

[1] Because, "to admit the lawfulness of holding an exposition of an Article of the Creed, contradictory of the essential meaning

And yet I could not but acknowledge that the
power which makes this decision is one fully competent to make it. It is that power to which the
Anglican Church first submitted itself in 1534, and
finally in 1559. It is the power under which it
has lived three hundred years, and by whose grant
it holds all its property. It is the power to which,
during all that time, its Clergy have sworn obedience, as " Supreme Governor;" and the nature of

of that Article, is in truth and in fact to abandon that Article;"
and "inasmuch as the Faith is one, and rests upon one principle
of authority, the conscious, deliberate, and wilful abandonment of
the essential meaning of an Article of the Creed destroys the
divine foundation upon which alone the entire Faith is pro-
pounded by the Church;" and "any portion of the Church,
which does so abandon the essential meaning of an Article of the
Creed, forfeits not only the Catholic doctrine in that Article, but
also the office and authority to witness and teach as a member
of the Universal Church."

Propositions signed by thirteen most distinguished names:

H. E. MANNING, M.A., *Archdeacon of Chichester*.
ROBERT J. WILBERFORCE, M.A., *Archdeacon of the East
Riding*.
THOMAS THORP, B.D., *Archdeacon of Bristol*.
W. H. MILL, D.D., *Regius Professor of Hebrew, Cambridge*.
E. B. PUSEY, D.D., *Regius Professor of Hebrew, Oxford*.
JOHN KEBLE, M.A., *Vicar of Hursley*.
W. DODSWORTH, M.A., *Perpetual Curate of Christ Church,
St. Pancras*.
W. J. E. BENNETT, M.A., *Perpetual Curate of St. Paul's,
Knightsbridge*.
H. W. WILBERFORCE, M.A., *Vicar of East Farleigh*.
JOHN C. TALBOT, M.A., *Barrister-at-law*.
RICHARD CAVENDISH, M.A.
EDWARD BADELEY, M.A., *Barrister-at-law*.
JAMES R. HOPE, D.C.L., *Barrister-at-law*.

Supremacy is, that what is subject to it cannot call
it in question.   It is the power which not only
nominates, but institutes, Bishops; erects, divides,
alters, and extinguishes bishoprics; causes Convocation to be summoned, or not to be summoned;
to transact, or not to transact business; confirms,
or does not confirm its acts; and, in short, the
power which constitutes the distinctive character
of the Anglican Communion, as to its government,
making it to differ both from the Catholic Church
and all Protestant sects.   Lastly, it is the power
which alone makes it a whole, the Cathedra Petri
of Anglicanism.

For all these reasons, it is a power which binds
the Anglican Church, its Clergy, and its Laity, as
a whole and as individuals; and accordingly a
power by the rightness or wrongness of whose decision in matters of faith the conscience of every
one in that communion, and his state before God,
is touched.

Now, to submit to this particular decision, I
must resign every principle of faith as a Christian,
as well as every feeling of honour as a freeman ;—
I would as soon sacrifice to Jupiter, or worship
Buddha, or again, take my faith from the civil
power ;—and to remain in the Anglican Communion is to submit to it.

But in the meantime the nearer consideration
of the Royal Supremacy had opened my mind to

comprehend the nature of its great antagonist, the
Primacy of S. Peter's See. For, as has been said,
the former consists in supremacy of jurisdiction,
whether viewed as deciding in the last resort upon
doctrine, and this as well legislatively, by giving
license to summon convocation, and by confirming
its acts, as judicially, in matters of appeal ; or as
giving mission and authority to exercise their
powers to all Bishops. Now, it was plain that
such a supremacy must exist somewhere in every
system. And immediately there followed the
question, What is that *somewhere* in the Church
Catholic? I could not even imagine any answer,
save that it was S. Peter's Chair. And then I saw
that the contest in Church history really lay not
between Ultramontane and Gallican opinions, but
between the liberty, independence, and spirituality
of Christ's Church on the one hand, or on its being
made a servile instrument of State government on
the other : between a divine and a human Church.
And now I went over again the testimonies of antiquity which I had before put together, and many
others besides ; and I found that one or two con-
fusions and incoherencies of mind—especially the
not understanding accurately the distinction between the power of Order and the power of Jurisdiction, and their consequences—had alone prevented
my seeing, not merely a Primacy of divine institution, but how full, complete, and overwhelming was

the testimony of the Church before the division of
the East and West to the Supremacy of S. Peter's
See, *as at present claimed*, the very same, and no
other. I had it proved to me by the evidence of
unnumbered witnesses, that the charge of such
Supremacy being originated by the false decretals
of Isidore Mercator was a most groundless, I fear
also, a most malignant and treacherous imputation.
And, moreover, I felt convinced that those who
deny the Papal Supremacy must, if they are honest
men, cease to study history, or at least begin their
acquaintance with Christianity at the sixteenth
century. Also that they must be content with a
dead Church, and no Creed.

When I had come to this conclusion, it became
a matter of absolute necessity and conscience to
act upon it, to resign my office and function of
teaching in the Anglican Church, and not only so,
but to leave that communion itself, in which, so far
from being able "to hold and teach all doctrine
which the undivided Church always held," I could
no longer teach, save as an "open question" (from
which degradation may God preserve me!), that
very primary doctrine which stands at the commencement of the spiritual life.

I leave therefore the Anglican Communion, not
simply because it is involved in heresy[1] by the

---

[1] See Archdeacon Manning's last pamphlet: "If there be,
therefore, such a thing as material heresy, it is the doctrine which

decision of Her Majesty in Council, but because that Royal Supremacy, in virtue of which Her Majesty decides at all in matters of doctrine, is a power utterly incompatible with the existence of the Church of God, and because Anglicanism, as a whole, has not only tampered with and corrupted the entire body of doctrine which concerns the Church and the Sacraments, but, as a living system, is based upon the denial of that Primacy of S. Peter's See to which I find Holy Scripture and the Church of the East and West bearing witness; and which I believe, on their authority, to have been established by Christ Himself as the Rock and immovable foundation of His Church, her safeguard from heresy and dissolution.

My last act as an Anglican, and my last *duty* to Anglicanism, is to set forth, as I do in the following pages, what has induced me to leave it.

has now received the sanction of the law " (p. 43). But the Anglican Episcopate has met upon this doctrine, considered, and *done nothing;* and so, *as a whole,* accepts it; nor has the Church, *as a whole,* rejected it ; only individuals have protested, and this in a far smaller number than those who have acquiesced in it. What is wanting to make it, as respects the communion itself, not only material, but formal heresy ?

CONTENTS.

THE SEE OF S. PETER.

SECTION I.

CHRISTIANITY is now more than eighteen hundred years old; and when we look around we find it planted, and more or less flourishing, among all the nations of the earth which are conspicuous for their power, their knowledge, and their civilisation. This common term Christianity distinguishes them broadly, but decisively, from all other nations outside of its pale. But a second glance makes it necessary to analyse this term itself; for it shows a great variety of differences in the religious belief and spiritual government of those whom we have thus classed together. About two-thirds in number of all calling themselves Christians are closely united under one head, whom they believe to be of divine institution—namely, the Bishop of Rome, the successor of S. Peter—and in one belief and one communion, of which that Bishop is the special bond. Of the remaining third part, two-thirds, again, profess a belief very nearly, save in one point, identical with the former, but distinguished in that they do not now acknowledge the Bishop of Rome

I

as the bond of their unity, though they freely admit
that he once stood at the head of that patriarchal
system of government which they still maintain.
These form the Oriental communion, embracing
the Greek and Russian Churches. Of other Eastern
sects it is not necessary here to speak. The rest,
forming the other third of this latter third, or one
ninth, numerically, of all Christians, may be classed
together as the Protestant, or Anglo-German phase
of Christianity. Most deeply opposed, in many of
their tenets, and in their whole tone of thinking and
feeling, to the last-mentioned communion, they yet
agree with it in rejecting the headship of S. Peter's
successor, and indeed are wont to add every con-
tumelious epithet which language can supply to the
claim of authority which he puts forth and exercises.
Not, however, that this Anglo-German Christianity
is united itself as to its spiritual government, or even
as to its belief. For whereas in England, and
partly in America, it is governed by Bishops, in
Prussia and Scotland, and again in the United
States, it has thrown off such control. Nor, again,
that its component portions have one creed, for it
has been found impossible to draw up articles of
belief to which they could all agree. Nevertheless,
this Anglo-German Christianity may be called one
mass, for it broke off, or at least was severed, at the
same time, from the great communion first mentioned, which still acknowledges the headship of
S. Peter's successor. And with many minor
diversities and gradations it has in common certain fundamental principles; such as the entire

rejection, in some portions of it, and in others the attenuation, of the doctrine of sacramental Grace, and in all, the maiming of that great sacramental system to which all the rest of Christianity adheres; and again, which is a part of the above, a denial that the spiritual government of the Church is lodged by a divine succession in certain *persons*. This idea, in some of its portions, as in Prussia, and in the Protestant sects of America, is utterly rejected; in others, as the Anglican Church, made an open question, it being notorious that part of its clergy consider such a notion a corruption of Christianity, while part as warmly maintain it to be necessary for the Church's existence. Again, all are united in rejecting the Roman view of the great mystery of the Real Presence, and of that reverence to Saints which flows forth from it, such as the ascription of miraculous effects to their relics, and of such prevailing power in their intercessions that they may lawfully and profitably be asked to pray for us. Perhaps this peculiarity of mind may be summed up in its most remarkable instance. For whereas that before-mentioned great Roman Communion, and no less the Eastern, is distinguished by a very special and wholly singular love and reverence towards the most Blessed Virgin Mary, as the Mother of God our Saviour; whereas all hearts within it are so penetrated with the thought of her divine maternity, that they cannot behold our Lord in His infancy, without seeing Him borne in His mother's arms; nor gaze upon Him suffering on the cross, without the thought of His mother transfixed with sorrow at His feet, so that He and she are indivisibly bound together, on Earth in the days of His flesh, in Heaven at the right hand of God, and the mystery of our redemption, completely accomplished in Him, yet enfolds her as the instrument of His incarnation, has an office and a function for her ; whereas these are daily household thoughts, and the dearest of all sympathies, in minds of the Roman and the Eastern Communion, the Anglo-German phase of Christianity is quite united in looking upon this reverence and love to the Blessed Virgin as dangerous, and tending to idolatry, and derogatory to our Lord.

On the whole, then, we may set down the actually existing Christianity as divided into three great portions : the Roman Catholic, united in government and belief, and comprehending two-thirds of the whole ;

The Oriental, with the Russian, and the sects parted from it ;

The Protestant, or Anglo-German.

At this moment, then, a variety of nations, having the most various worldly interests, and the most distinct national, moral, and political character, are united in acknowledging, as the head of their religion, the successor of S. Peter, the Bishop of Rome. And after all the divisions and conflicts of Christianity within itself, two-thirds of all professing it are still of one mind, and more than one hundred and sixty millions of souls, by the confession of an adversary, see, in the divine framework of the visible Church which holds them together, one mainspring and motive power, controlling and harmonising all the rest : in the circle which embraces them and the world, one centre, S. Peter's See, the throne of the Fisherman, built by the Carpenter's Son.

The Anglican Church professes a belief in Episcopacy ; it is not unworthy of its attention, that of about eleven hundred Bishops now in the world (admitting the claim of one hundred of Anglican descent) eight hundred own allegiance to the Pope. If a General Council could sit, there would be no doubt on which side the vast majority would be.

If nations could represent the Church, as at the Council of Constance, there would be as little uncertainty in the result.

Such is the aspect of things in the present day ; but Christianity numbers more than eighteen hundred years. " Remember the days of old: consider the years of many generations. Ask thy father, and he will show thee : thy elders, and they will tell thee." Of eighteen hundred years let us go back three hundred and fifty, from 1850 to 1500.

Where is the Anglo-German phase of Christianity ? What nations did it number ? What powers of the world did it set in motion ? *It was yet to come.* Its principles, indeed, had lurked in the restless mind of Wickliffe ; had seemed, and but seemed, to expire in the ashes of Huss. It was darkly and mistily agitating unquiet thoughts in England and Germany, flying, like a bird of ill omen, round the proud towers of the Church of

God, or festering in corners of corruption over high powers misused. But in fixed shape and consistency, as yet *it was not*. That which now claims to be the pure and reformed Church *had no existence*. The Anglo-Saxon mind had been formed and grown up under the control of S. Peter's See: and the country of Luther still with one voice reverenced that Winfrid, who, from the island won to the cross by S. Gregory, went forth to his successor, begged his apostolic blessing, and planted in Mayence the crosier which he had received from Rome. The Churches of Germany and England owed to the Papal See their whole organisation, and had subsisted, the one for eight hundred, the other for nine hundred years, under that fostering power. The claim which Germany and England now reject was then written on every page of the ecclesiastical legislation of those countries. Their first Metropolitans had received their jurisdiction from the Pope; the diocese of every German and English Bishop had been defined by the Pope; the institution of every Bishop to his see had been received from the Pope, and at the most awful moment of his life, every spiritual ruler had sworn that he would uphold the See of S. Peter, and its occupant, "principem episcopalis coronæ." [1]

Go back but three centuries and a half, and this ninth part of Christianity—this busy, prying, restless mind, which criticises everything and believes

[1] Edict of the Emperor Valentinian, A.D. 445.

nothing; pulls down, but never builds up; analyses the principle of life, and by the dissection kills it—which treats the Holy Scripture as the ploughboy treated the watch, pulls it to pieces to look at its mechanism, and then wonders that it will not go; which grudges to men even the Apostles' Creed, and will not let them hold that there is one baptism for the remission of sins, but on condition that they communicate with those who deny it; this spirit, which, in its most advanced development, casts Christianity itself into the alembic, and makes it come out a volatile essence of pantheism—in one word, Protestantism, *was not.*

Thus those who most bitterly reject the Papal Supremacy as an usurpation of late times are found themselves to have begun to exist ages after the supposed corruption which they denounce.

But there are older, more consistent, more dignified deniers of the Pope's claim than those who date from the Reformation.

To meet these, let us go back, instead of three hundred and fifty, a thousand years. In the year 850, not only Italy, and Spain, and Gaul, and Britain, and Germany, but the Roman Empire of the East, the Patriarchs of Constantinople, Alexandria, Antioch, Jerusalem, and their subject Bishops and people, acknowledged S. Peter's successor, without a doubt and without a murmur, as "chief pastor of the Church which is under Heaven."[1] I shall have occasion to bring forward

---

[1] S. Theodore Studites, Abbot of Constantinople. Baronius, A.D. 809, n. 14.

presently testimonies from the highest authorities among them, and from their Bishops assembled in Ecumenical Council; testimonies of the complete obedience which they yielded to the Pope's Supremacy, as well in matters of faith as of discipline.

But in 850 modern Europe was at least in part constituted—the foundations of present legislation had been laid—some thrones, still existing, had been raised; the north had cast forth its hordes whom the Church was moulding into empires, and out of freemen making legislators: Charlemagne had been crowned Emperor of the Romans before S. Peter's shrine, by the hands of S. Peter's successor, and Alfred was just about to receive his first education at Rome under S. Leo the Fourth. Let us go back another five hundred years, into that old Roman civilisation, when the children of Constantine sat on his throne, and Athanasius was being tried for his faith. A General Council is assembled at Sardica, A.D. 347, and it recognises S. Peter's successor as in full, time-honoured possession of his supreme power. It directs, not as a new thing, nor as the recognition of a new power, but what was "best and most fitting," as being in accordance with all ancient usage, that all Bishops, in case of difficulty, "should refer *to the head*, that is, *the See of the Apostle Peter.*"

And the first Council in which the whole Church was represented, the Nicene Council, famous to all ages, stated, not as granting a favour, but bearing witness to a fact, and acknowledging a power existing from the very first, without attempting to

define it—for indeed that power was neither derived
from its gift, nor subject to its control—" the Roman
Church always had the Primacy."[1]

If, then, two-thirds of all existing Christians
acknowledge still the Pope's Supremacy, and if the
countries forming the remaining third did formerly,
and that for many hundred years, acknowledge it,
certainly it can fairly claim the right of a *power in
possession*; it can throw the *burden of proof* on those
who deny it. And this is a consideration of some
importance. A power now exists in most active
and manifold operation at the very centre of the
Church of Christ—a supreme, controlling, harmonising, conservative, unitive, defining power, in that
mighty empire of thought which our Lord has set
up. Who put it there? It answers: Our Lord
Himself. And it points to a great number of proofs,
bearing witness to its existence, in the history of

---

[1] That is, as quoted by the Papal Legates at the Council of
Chalcedon. If it be objected that the Greek copies do not begin
the 6th canon, which is the one in question, with this heading, as
was observed by the Archdeacon of Constantinople at the Council
of Chalcedon, yet at the same time neither he nor any one else
denied the fact that the Nicene Council acknowledged this
Primacy of Rome; nay, the 29th canon of the Council of Chalcedon, which the Greek party was at the time trying to pass, and
which the Popes would never ratify, recognised the Primacy of
Rome at least *de facto* ; nor was there any one in that Council
who even pretended that it had arisen between A.D. 325 and A.D.
451. Whatever, therefore, be the true reading of the much-
debated 6th canon of the Nicene Council, which seems not even
yet to be settled, so much, at least, is clear, that the Primacy of
Rome was admitted to be *recognised* by it, which is all that is
asserted in the text. (*Note to Second Edition.*)

10 THE PRIMACY OF S. PETER

eighteen hundred years. Now these proofs are of
very various cogency. No one of them perhaps
defines, or could define, the whole range of the
power; but one exhibits it in this particular, and
another in that: for instance, one ancient saint declares " that it is necessary that every Church should
agree with the Roman, on account of its superiority
of headship ; " another, that " unity begins from it ; "
a third, that " where Peter is, there is the Church ; "
a fourth, that " the headship of the Apostolic See
has always flourished in it."[1] Now it is plain that
these expressions want a key. And such is supplied
by the present existence of that power. The fair
and candid mind will see in them much more even
than they at first sight convey : for it was not
the purpose of the writers at the moment to *define*
the power to which they were alluding, any more
than those living under the supremacy of the British
monarchy, in any casual mention of it, would do
otherwise than refer to it as an existing thing.
If such attributes, then, of the Roman See, separately
mentioned by different Fathers, all fit into, and are
explained by, an existing power, and, when put
together, here one and there another, exhibit, more
or less, such a power, it is fair so to interpret them,
and to infer that the power which we now see
existed then. For attaining the truth, it is most
necessary to begin by studying it under right conditions. In interpreting expressions there is often
a great difference between what they *must* and

[1] 1, S. Irenæus; 2, S. Cyprian; 3, S. Ambrose; 4, S. Augustine.
(*Note to Second Edition.*)

what they *may* mean : now an existing power has a right, in such cases as these, that they should be interpreted in its favour.

For consider what a phenomenon, wholly without a parallel, this power, as at present existing, exhibits.

Not merely is it older than all the monarchies of Europe ; little is it to say that it has watched over their first rudiments, fostered their growth, assisted their development, maintained their maturity ; it has been further upheld by a deep belief, shared in common by many various nations, older in each of them than their existence as nations, and continuing on through the lapse of ages, while almost everything else in those nations has changed ; not only does it rule, claiming an equal and paternal sway over all, in spite of their various jealousies, their national antagonism, or their diverse temperament, so that German and Italian, who love not each other, Pole and Spaniard, who are so dissimilar, have yet in their faith a common Father ; but, moreover, every circumstance of the world has altered, and society gone round its whole cycle, from a corrupt heathen civilisation, through a wild barbarism conflicting with Christianity, into wise and venerable polities built upon the Church, and having its life infused into their own, while all throughout a line of old men has been on the banks of the Tiber, ruling this huge and many-membered Christian Commonwealth, not by the arm of the flesh, but by the word of the Spirit. Nations fought and conquered, or were subdued ; populations were

changed, and races engrafted. German and
Italian, Frank and Gaul, Goth and Iberian, Saxon
and Briton, Slavonian and Hun, were dashed together. There were centuries of bitter wrong—
the pangs of Europe hastening to the birth. But
a presiding spirit was there too, and brooded over
all—a spirit of unity, order, and love. At last the
darkness broke, and it was found that these wild
nations one and all, recognised the keys of Peter,
and felt the sword of Paul. An omen of this
victory had appeared in early times. S. Leo set
forth the true doctrine of the Incarnation; the
Church listened, and was saved from a heresy
already half imposed upon her by the civil power
of the Eastern empire. The Western empire
trembled at the approach of Attila, and the same
Leo went forth to meet the barbarian, who was
awed by the simple majesty of his presence, and
the power of God in the person of His chief
minister.

Fourteen hundred years have passed, and Leo's
successor still sits upon his throne; hundreds of
bishops, and millions of faithful, still believe that
his voice sets forth and protects the true faith in
every emergent heresy; and that wild force which
Attila wielded has been tamed to the dominion of
law, in that long course of intervening ages, by the
power which Leo represented. Yet, great as was
his influence as head of the Church, still incomparably greater now is the authority of his successor
amongst the nations of the earth, after all defec-
tions, amid all the unbelief of these latter times,

when "many run to and fro, and knowledge is increased," and perilous powers are in motion and combination,—powers which seek to substitute the human intellect, with the arts and commodities of life springing from it, for the grace of God healing the nations, and the truth which He has committed to the guardianship of His mystical Body.

Manners, races, empires, have changed and passed away, but what S. Prosper sung in 431 is as true now :

" Sedes Roma Petri, quæ pastoralis honoris
Facta caput mundo, quicquid non possidet armis
Religione tenet."

S. Augustine, at the end of the fourth century, pointed to the line of Bishops descending from the very seat of Peter, to whom the Lord intrusted His sheep to be fed, as holding him in the Catholic Church. It was a cogent argument then ; but what is it now, when fourteen centuries and a half have added more than two hundred successors to that chair, and more than forty generations have encircled it with their homage ?

Is it possible for an *usurpation* to subsist under such conditions ? Will many various nations agree that the head of their religion should be external to themselves ? Will the members of these various and jealous nations, who are equal in their episcopal power, allow a *brother* to arrange their precedence, control their actions, terminate their disputes, rule them as one flock, and that for fifteen centuries together ?

Or where shall we seek the foundation of such a power? The Church bears witness to it, but did not create it. Councils acknowledge it, but it is before councils. The first of them said: "The Roman Church always had the Primacy." Who is sufficient to create such an institution, and to maintain it? to take a common pebble that lay at his feet, and build on it a pyramid that should last for ever; on which for evermore the rain should descend, the floods fall, and the winds blow, and all the power of the evil one be exerted in vain? One alone, surely. So this authority itself declares. So the Church itself witnesses. So unnumbered saints from age to age proclaim. That One who said, "Let there be light," and "This is My Body," said also, "Thou art Peter, and upon this rock I will build My Church, and the gates of Hell shall not prevail against it. And I will give unto thee the keys of the kingdom of Heaven; and whatsoever thou shalt bind on Earth shall be bound in Heaven; and whatsoever thou shalt loose on Earth shall be loosed in Heaven."

But of this we must speak more in detail.

SECTION II.

THE SCRIPTURAL PROOF OF THE PRIMACY.

" IN *our* life," said S. Bernard, "we seem to do, so far as our own purpose is concerned, many things by chance, and many by necessity ; but Christ, the Power of God and the Wisdom of God, could be subject to neither of these. For what necessity could force God's Power, or what should God's Wisdom do by chance ? Wherefore all things whatsoever He spake, whatsoever He did, whatsoever He suffered, doubt not to have proceeded from His will, full of mysteries, full of salvation." [1]

If such thoughts are becoming in respect of all the words which God spake on earth in the days of His flesh, they apply with peculiar force to those few and short sentences wherein He summed up the authority which He was conferring on His Apostles for the institution and edification of His Church. They are creative words, full of power, stretching through all time, each one in itself a prophecy, a miracle, and a manifold mystery.

Assuredly, therefore, not without a special meaning were some things said to all the Apostles in common, and some to S. Peter alone.

[1] *In Festo Ascensionis*, Serm. iv.

Let us distinguish these.

And, further, let us distinguish the *promise* from the *fulfilment*.

Now there was one single *promise*, respecting the government of His Church, made by our Lord to S. Peter singly, and another made to all the Apostles together, including Peter. They have a close connection with each other, and the better to see their force let us put them in parallel columns:

TO PETER.	TO THE APOSTLES.
" 1. I say also unto thee, that thou art Peter, and upon this Rock I will build My Church.	
" 2. And the gates of Hell shall not prevail against it.	
" 3. And I will give unto thee the keys of the kingdom of Heaven,	
" 4. And whatsoever thou shalt bind on Earth shall be bound in Heaven, and whatsoever thou shalt loose on Earth shall be loosed in Heaven."	" Verily I say unto you, Whatsoever ye shall bind on Earth shall be bound in Heaven, and whatsoever ye shall loose on Earth shall be loosed in Heaven."

Here it will be observed that four things are *first* promised to Peter alone, the fourth of which is *afterwards* promised to the Apostles together, including Peter.

And the *fulfilment* of this fourth promise is made likewise to all the Apostles together, thus :
" Peace be unto you: as My Father hath sent Me, even so send I you.
" And when He had said this, He breathed on them, and saith unto them, Receive ye the Holy Ghost : whosoever sins ye remit, they are remitted unto them ; and whosoever sins ye retain, they are retained."
The other passages which express powers given to the Apostles in common are these :
1 Cor. xi. 23-25 : "The Lord Jesus the same night in which He was betrayed took bread ; and when He had given thanks, He brake it, and said, Take, eat : this is My Body, which is given for you : *this do in remembrance of Me.* After the same manner also He took the cup when He had supped, saying : This cup is the new testament in My Blood : *this do ye, as oft as ye drink it, in remembrance of Me.*" See also Luke xxii. 19.
Matt. xxviii. 18-20 : "Jesus came and spake unto them, saying : All power is given unto Me in Heaven and in Earth. ,Go ye therefore, and teach all nations, baptising them in the name of the Father, and of the Son, and of the Holy Ghost : teaching them to observe all things whatsoever I have commanded you : and, lo, I am with you alway, even unto the end of the world. Amen."
Mark xvi. 15 : " And He said unto them : Go ye into all the world, and preach the Gospel to every creature."
Luke xxiv. 49 : " And, behold, I send the pro-

mise of My Father upon you : but tarry ye in the city of Jerusalem until ye be endued with power from on high."

Acts i. 4, 5, 8 : " Being assembled together with them, He commanded them that they should not depart from Jerusalem, but wait for the promise of the Father, which, saith He, ye have heard of Me. For John truly baptised with water ; but ye shall be baptised with the Holy Ghost not many days hence.

" Ye shall receive power, after that the Holy Ghost is come upon you : and ye shall be witnesses unto Me both in Jerusalem, and in all Judea, and in Samaria, and unto the uttermost part of the earth."

We have seen that three out of four promises made to Peter singly were not made to the other Apostles, and two remarkable passages remain, which belong to Peter only.

Our Lord, when all the Apostles were around Him, at the time of His passion, singling out Peter, said to him : " Simon, Simon, behold Satan hath desired to have *you*, that he may sift you as wheat : but I have prayed for *thee ;* and thou, when thou art converted, *confirm thy brethren.*"

And *after* He had delivered His commission to the Apostles assembled together, and sent them, as He was sent from the Father, bestowing on them the power to forgive sins, all which involved their Apostolate, He took an occasion, when Peter, James, and John, His most favoured disciples, and four others, were together, to address S. Peter singly in very memorable words.   John xxi. 15 :

" So when they had dined, Jesus saith to Simon

Peter: Simon, son of Jonas, lovest thou Me *more than these?* He saith unto Him: Yea, Lord, Thou knowest that I love Thee. He saith unto him: Feed My lambs (*Βόσκε τὰ ἀρνία μου*).

" He saith to him again the second time : Simon, son of Jonas, lovest thou Me ? He saith unto Him : Yea, Lord, Thou knowest that I love Thee. He saith unto him : Feed My sheep (*Ποίμαινε τὰ πρόβατά μου*).

"He saith unto him the third time: Simon, son of Jonas, lovest thou Me ? Peter was grieved because He said unto him the third time : Lovest thou Me ? And he said unto Him : Lord, Thou knowest all things : Thou knowest that I love Thee. Jesus saith unto him : Feed My sheep " (*Βόσκε τὰ πρόβατά μου*).

These are all the passages, respecting their own office and functions, spoken either to the Apostles in common, or to Peter singly ; very few out of which to construct the government of the universal Church, were the Constructor less than God, but sufficient for Him whose word creates. Let us now sum up the powers conveyed in them : first those given to the Apostles in common; then those peculiar to Peter.

Of those given to the Apostles in common, the following are *ordinary*, that is, requisite for the perpetual government of the Church :

1. Offering the holy Sacrifice—" This do (*τοῦτο ποιεῖτε, hoc facite*, the sacrificial words) in remembrance of Me." In other words, Power over the natural Body of Christ.

2. Forgiving sins, in the Sacrament of Penance—
"Whosesoever sins ye remit," etc.   That is, Power
over the mystical Body of Christ.

These make up the Priesthood.

3. Baptising—"Baptising them," etc.

4. Teaching and administering all other Sacraments and rites, and enjoining obedience to them—
"Teaching them to observe all things," etc.

5. Inflicting   and   removing ⎧ "Whatsoever
censures—   ⎨ ye   shall   bind,"
6. Binding by laws—   ⎩   etc.

7. The presence of Christ with them in this
office to the end—"Lo, I am with you alway."

These involve the Episcopate. ·

The following are *extraordinary*, making up, in
fact, the Apostolate, as distinguished from the
Episcopate :

8. Immediate institution by Christ—"As My
Father hath sent Me," etc.

9. Universal   mission—"Go   ye   into   all   the
world."

Now all these powers S. Peter shared in common
with the other Apostles, and therefore in all these
they were equal ; but the following are peculiar to
himself :

1. He is made the Rock, or foundation of the
Church, next after Christ, and singly—"Thou art
Peter, and upon this Rock I will build My Church."

2. To the Church, thus founded on him, perpetual continuance and victory are guaranteed—
"The gates of Hell shall not prevail against it."

3. The keys of the kingdom of Heaven, that is,

the symbol of supreme power, the mastership over the Lord's House, the guardianship of the Lord's City, are committed to him alone—" To thee will I give the keys of the kingdom of Heaven."

4. The power of binding and loosing sins, of inflicting and removing censures, of enacting spiritual laws, given to him elsewhere *with* the Apostles, is here given to him singly—" And whatsoever thou shalt bind," etc.

5. The power of confirming his brethren, because his own faith should never fail.

6. The supreme pastorship of all Christ's flock is bestowed on him—" Feed My lambs—be shepherd over My sheep—feed My sheep."

Thus, comparing together what was given to the Apostles in common, and what was given to Peter singly, we find that :

1. He received many things alone—they nothing without him.

2. His powers can be exercised only by one—theirs by many.

3. His powers include theirs—not theirs his.

4. The ordinary government of the Church, promised and prefigured in the keys of the kingdom of Heaven, conveyed and summed up in " Feed My sheep," that is, the pastoral office—radiates from his person ; the Episcopate is folded up in the Primacy.

Moreover, as to the continuance and descent of these powers, the same principle which leads all Churchmen to believe that the ordinary powers bestowed on the Apostles in common for the good

of the Church are continued on to those who
govern the Church for ever, leads also to the
belief that the power bestowed on Peter likewise
for the good of the Church continues on to his
successors in like manner. Indeed, part of the
promise is express on this head, assigning perpetual continuance to the Church founded on
Peter.

Further, we learn in what respects the Apostles
were equal to Peter, and in what he was superior
to them.

They were equal in the powers of the Episcopate ;

They were equal also in those of the Apostolate,
superadded to the former, that is, immediate institution by Christ, and universal mission ;

They were inferior to him in one point only,
which made up his Primacy, namely, that they
must exercise all these powers in union with him,
and in dependence on him : he had *singly* what
they had *collectively* with him.   He had promised
and engaged to him, *first* and *alone*, the supreme
government, a portion of which was afterwards
promised to them with him ; and after the Apostolate, granted to them all in common, he had the
supervision of all intrusted to him alone.   For
even they were committed to his charge in the
words, " Feed My sheep."   And so he alone was
the doorkeeper ; he alone the shepherd of the fold ;
he alone the rock on which even they, as well as
all other Christians, were built ; in one word, he
was their head, and so his Primacy is an *essential*

part, nay, the crown and completion of the divine government of the Church; for the Body without a Head is no Body.

Thus were they all doctors of the whole world, as S. Cyril and S. Chrysostom tell us, yet under one, the leader of the band.

They could, and did, exercise jurisdiction, erect Bishops, and plant Churches, in all parts of the world, but it was in union with Peter, and in obedience to him.

His Primacy, then, consisted not in a superiority of *order*, but in a superiority of *jurisdiction*.

After the departure of the Apostles, this superiority of jurisdiction in the Primacy would be seen more clearly. For they communicated to none that universal mission which they themselves received from Christ, the Bishops whom they ordained having only a restricted field in which they exercised their powers; and it is manifest that our Lord in person instituted no Bishops after them. Thus these two privileges of the Apostolate, universal mission, and immediate institution by Christ, dropped. But S. Peter's Primacy, being distinct from his Apostolate, continued on. There was one still necessary to bear the keys of the kingdom of Heaven, and to feed all the sheep of the Lord's flock. That power, first promised, and last given, to Peter, the crown and key-stone of the arch, that which makes the whole Church one flock, was an universal Episcopate. Thus the Primacy is jurisdictional, with regard to all Bishops, as it was with regard to the Apostles; and two powers emerge, of divine institution, for the government of the Church to the end of time—the Primacy and the Episcopate.

And the power thus given to Peter singly, *in promise*, that he should be the rock, the foundation of the Church, never to be moved from its place, the bearer of the keys, binding and loosing all in heaven and earth, in *fulfilment*, that he should be the one shepherd charged with the care of all the sheep,—this power is, of its own nature, *supreme*. It embraces the whole flock, as well as the different sheep; the Church collectively, as well as its members distributively. It reaches to every need which can arise. Once grasp its true nature, and you see that it cannot be limited by any power over which it is appointed itself to rule. Yet is it tempered by that one condition laid upon it by our Lord at its institution, " Simon, son of Jonas, lovest thou Me more than these ? " more than James, and more than John. This superior love is indeed needed by him who wields such a power in a kingdom built upon that love which sacrificed itself for the world ; and that power itself is given for edification and not for destruction, but for that very reason is supreme, and answerable to Him alone who created it, and willed it to represent His Person upon earth.

All came from the Person of God the Word Incarnate ; all, therefore, is upheld from above, and not from below. All proceeded from One ; all is concentrated in One. The Father is supreme, but he is a Father.

Now, in all this I have hitherto gone on the mere words of Scripture, which are so plain, so coherent, so decisive, that I cannot imagine a candid mind drawing any other conclusion from them.[1]

It is another argument, and no less a truth, that this view alone supplies a key to all antiquity. Thus alone does the history of the Church become intelligible. A power of divine institution, deposited from the beginning within it, is seen to grow with its growth, to be the root on which it is planted, and the spring of its organisation ; to enfold in itself, and develop from itself, all other powers, imparting force to each, and harmony to all.

And now I will select, out of ancient and modern times, the testimony of two great Bishops to this

[1] The writer has been censured by members of that party in the Anglican Church to which he formerly belonged, for saying that " he cannot conceive any candid mind drawing any other conclusion " from these texts, as if he had in so saying condemned himself for not having formerly drawn such conclusion from these very texts. But in point of fact *a modern contradictory tradition, inculcating as a first principle of belief that the Primacy of S. Peter, as continued in the Pope, is a corruption of Christianity,* had then possession of his mind, as it has possession of so many Protestant minds at present, and prevented his even studying what was said in Holy Writ with regard to this particular subject. Such a tradition makes a mind incapable of exercising candour, however much it may desire to do so. Though Protestants profess to go by the Bible alone, probably not one Protestant in a million has ever attempted to judge dispassionately of what is said in Scripture to Peter and to the other Apostles as to their power of governing the Church. It was already a ruled point in their minds. *(Note to Second Edition.)*

interpretation of Holy Scripture. One shall be the representative of the Fathers, the other of the present Church.

More than fourteen hundred years ago, the great Pope Leo, in the midst of an assembly of Bishops, collected from all Italy to commemorate the anniversary of his pontificate, thus exhibited the mind of the Church in the middle of the fifth century respecting the See of Peter:

" Although, then, beloved, our partaking in that gift (of unity) be a great subject for common joy, yet it were a better and more excellent course of rejoicing, if ye rest not in the consideration of our humility ; more profitable and more worthy by far it is to raise the mind's eye unto the contemplation of the most blessed Apostle Peter's glory, and to celebrate this day chiefly in the honour of him *who was watered with streams so copious from the very fountain of all graces, that while nothing has passed to others without his participation, yet he received many special privileges of his own.* The Word made flesh already was dwelling in us, and Christ had given up Himself whole to restore the race of man. Nothing was unordered to His wisdom; nothing difficult to His power. Elements were obeying, spirits ministering, angels serving ; it was impossible that mystery could fail of its effect, in which the Unity and the Trinity of the Godhead itself was at once working. *And yet out of the whole world Peter alone is chosen to preside over the calling of all the Gentiles, and over all the Apostles and the collected Fathers of the Church ; so that, though there be among the people of God many priests and many shepherds, yet Peter rules all by immediate commission, whom Christ also rules by sovereign power.* Beloved, *it is a great and wonderful participation of His own power which the Divine condescendence gave to this man ; and if He willed that other rulers should enjoy aught together with him, yet never did He give, save through him, what He denied not to others.* In fine, the Lord asks all the Apostles what men think of Him ; and they answer in common so long as they set forth the doubtfulness of human ignorance. But when what the disciples think is required, he who is first in Apostolic dignity is first also in confession of the Lord. And when he had said : ' Thou art Christ, the Son of the living God,' Jesus answered him : ' Blessed art thou, Simon Bar-Jona, because flesh and blood hath not revealed it to thee, but My Father which is in Heaven : '—that is, Thou art blessed, because My Father hath taught thee ; nor hath opinion of the earth deceived thee, but inspiration from Heaven instructed thee ; and not flesh and blood hath shown Me to thee, but He whose only-begotten Son I am. ' And I,' saith He, ' say unto thee,'—that is, as My Father hath manifested to thee My Godhead, so I too make known unto thee thine own pre-eminence,—' For thou art Peter,' that is, whilst I am the immutable Rock ; I the Corner-Stone who make both one ; I the Foundation beside which no one can lay another ; *yet thou also art a Rock, because by My virtue thou art firmly planted, so that whatever is peculiar to Me by power, is to thee by participation common with Me,*—'and upon this Rock I will build My Church, and the gates of hell shall not prevail against it;'—on this strength, said He, I will build an eternal temple, and My Church, which in its height shall reach the Heaven, shall rise upon the firmness of this faith.

"This confession the gates of hell shall not restrain, nor the chains of death fetter; for that voice is the voice of life. And as it raises those who confess it unto heavenly places, so it plunges those who deny it into hell. Wherefore it is said to most blessed Peter: 'I will give to thee the keys of the kingdom of heaven, and whatsoever thou shalt bind on earth shall be bound in heaven; and whatsoever thou shalt loose on earth shall be loosed in heaven.' *The privilege of this power did indeed pass on to the other Apostles, and the order of this decree spread out to all the rulers of the Church, but not without purpose what is intended for all is put into the hands of one. For therefore is this intrusted to Peter singularly, because all the rulers of the Church are invested with the figure of Peter.* The privilege, therefore, of Peter remaineth, whereso-ever judgment is passed according to his equity. Nor can severity or indulgence be excessive, where nothing is bound, nothing loosed, save what blessed Peter either bindeth or looseth. Again, as that Passion drew on which was about to shake the firmness of His disciples, the Lord saith: 'Simon, Simon, behold Satan hath desired to have you, that he may sift you as wheat ; but I have prayed for thee, that thy faith fail not ; and when thou art converted, confirm thy brethren, that ye enter not into temptation.' The danger from the temptation of fear was common to all the Apostles, and they equally needed the help of divine protection, since the devil desired to dismay, to make a wreck of all : *and yet the Lord takes care of Peter in particular, and asks specially for the faith of Peter, as if the state of the rest would be more certain, if the mind of their chief were not overcome. So then in Peter the strength of all is fortified, and the help of Divine grace is so ordered that the stability which through Christ is given to Peter, through Peter is conveyed to the Apostles.*

"Since then, beloved, we see such a protection divinely granted to us, reasonably and justly do we rejoice in the merits.and dignity of our chief, rendering thanks to the Eternal King, our Redeemer, the Lord Jesus Christ, *for having given so great a power to him whom He made chief of the whole Church*, that if anything, even in our time, by us be rightly done and rightly ordered, it is to be ascribed to his working, to his guidance, unto whom it was said : 'And thou, when thou art converted, confirm thy brethren ;' and to whom the Lord, after His resurrection, in answer to the triple profession of eternal love, thrice said, with mystical intent : 'Feed My sheep.' And this, beyond a doubt, the pious shepherd does even now, and fulfils the charge of his Lord, confirming us with his exhortations, and not ceasing to pray for us, that we may be overcome by no temptation. But if, as we must believe, he every- where discharges this affectionate guardianship to all the people of God, how much more will he · condescend to grant his help unto us his children, among whom, on the sacred couch of his blessed repose, he resteth in the same flesh in which he ruled ! To him, therefore, let us ascribe this anni- versary day of us his servant, and this festival, by whose advocacy we have been thought worthy to share his seat itself, the grace of our Lord Jesus Christ helping us in all things, who liveth and reigneth with God the Father and the Holy Spirit, for ever and ever." [1]

I defer to a later place the proof how exactly all this accords with the doctrine of S. Augustine, and the Fathers who preceded him.

Now let us pass on through twelve centuries to another scene, where a Bishop, at the court of a sovereign intoxicated with power, and most jealous of his temporal rights as sovereign, set forth to the Gallican Episcopate solemnly assembled the doctrines to be gathered from these words of Scripture.

" Listen : this is the mystery of Catholic unity, and the immortal principle of the Church's beauty. True beauty comes from health ; what makes the Church strong, makes her fair : her unity makes her fair, her unity makes her strong. United from within by the Holy Spirit, she has besides a com-

---

[1] S. Leo, *Serm.* iv., tom. i. pp. 15-19.

mon bond of her outward communion, and must remain united by a government in which the authority of Jesus Christ is represented. Thus one unity guards the other, and, under the seal of ecclesiastical government, the unity of the spirit is preserved. What is this government? What is its form? Let us say nothing of ourselves ; let us open the Gospel; the Lamb has opened the seals of that sacred book, and the tradition of the Church has explained all.

"We shall find in the Gospel that Jesus Christ, willing to *commence* the mystery of unity in His Church, among all His disciples chose twelve; but that, willing to *consummate* the mystery of unity in the same Church, among the twelve He chose one. 'He called His disciples,' said the Gospel; here are all; 'and among them He chose twelve.' Here is a first separation, and the Apostles chosen. 'And these are the names of the twelve Apostles : the first, Simon, who is called Peter.' Here, in a second separation, S. Peter is set at the head, and called for that reason by the name of Peter, 'which Jesus Christ,' says S. Mark, 'had given him,' in order to prepare, as you will see, the work which He was proposing, to raise all His building on that stone.

" All this is yet but a commencement of the mystery of unity. Jesus Christ, in beginning it, still spoke to many : 'Go ye, preach ye ; I send you ;' but when He would put the last hand to the mystery of unity, He speaks no longer to many : He marks out Peter personally, and by the new

name which He has given him. It is One who
speaks to one : Jesus Christ the Son of God to
Simon son of Jonas ; Jesus Christ, who is the true
Stone, strong of Himself, to Simon, who is only
the stone by the strength which Jesus Christ im-
parts to him. It is to him that Christ speaks, and
in speaking acts on him, and stamps upon him
His own immovableness. 'And I,' He says, ' say
unto thee, thou art Peter ; and,' He adds, ' upon
this rock I will build My Church, and,' He con-
cludes, 'the gates of hell shall not prevail against
it.' To prepare him for that honour Jesus Christ,
who knows that faith in Himself is the foundation
of His Church, inspires Peter with a faith worthy
to be the foundation of that admirable building,
' Thou art the Christ, the Son of the living God.'
By that bold preaching of the faith he draws to
himself the inviolable promise which makes him
the foundation of the Church. The word of Jesus
Christ, who out of nothing makes what pleases
Him, gives this strength to a mortal. *Say not,
think not, that this ministry of S. Peter terminates
with him : that which is to serve for support to an
eternal Church can never have an end.* Peter will
live in his successors. Peter will always speak in
his chair. This is what the Fathers say. This is
what six hundred and thirty Bishops at the Council
of Chalcedon confirm.

" But consider briefly what follows—Jesus Christ
pursues His design ; and, after having said to
Peter, the eternal preacher of the faith, ' Thou art
Peter, and upon this rock I will build My Church,'

He adds: 'And I will give to thee the keys of the kingdom of heaven.' Thou, who hast the prerogative of preaching the faith, thou shalt have likewise the keys which mark the authority of government : 'What thou shalt bind on earth shall be bound in heaven : and what thou shalt loose on earth shall be loosed in heaven.' *All is subjected to these keys : all, my brethren, kings and nations, pastors and flocks :* we declare it with joy, for we love unity, and hold obedience to be our glory. It is Peter who is ordered first to love more than all the other Apostles, and then 'to feed,' and govern all, both 'the lambs and the sheep,' the young ones, and the mothers, and the pastors themselves : *pastors in regard to the people, and sheep in regard to Peter;* in him they honour Jesus Christ, confessing likewise that with reason greater love is asked of him, forasmuch as he has a greater dignity with a greater charge ; and that among us, under the discipline of a Master such as ours, according to His word it must be, that the first be as He, by charity the servant of all.

" Thus S. Peter appears the first in all things : the first to confess the faith ; the first in the obligation to exercise love ; the first of all the Apostles who saw Jesus Christ risen, as he was to be the first witness of it before all the people; the first when the number of the Apostles was to be filled up ; the first who confirmed the faith by a miracle ; the first to convert the Jews ; the first to receive the Gentiles ; the first everywhere.

" You have seen this unity in the Holy See,

would you see it in the whole episcopal order and college? Still it is in S. Peter that it must appear, and still in these words: 'Whatsoever thou shalt bind shall be bound; whatsoever thou shalt loose shall be loosed.' All the Popes and all the Holy Fathers have taught it with a common consent. Yes, my brethren, these great words, in which you have seen so clearly the Primacy of S. Peter, have set up Bishops, since the force of their ministry consists in binding or loosing those who believe or believe not their word. Thus this divine power of binding and loosing is a necessary annexment, and, as it were, the final seal of the preaching which Jesus Christ has intrusted to them; and you see, in passing, the whole order of ecclesiastical jurisdiction. Therefore, the same who said to Peter: 'Whatsoever thou shalt bind shall be bound; whatsoever thou shalt loose shall be loosed,' has said the same thing to all the Apostles, and has said to them, moreover: 'Whosesoever sins ye remit, they shall be remitted; and whosesoever sins ye retain, they shall be retained.' What is to bind, but to retain?' What to loose, but to remit? And the same who gives to Peter this power, gives it also with His own mouth to all the Apostles: 'As My Father hath sent Me, so,' says He, 'send I you.' A power better established, or a mission more immediate, cannot be seen. So He breathes equally on all. On all He diffuses the same Spirit with that breath, in saying: 'Receive ye the Holy Ghost,' and the rest that we have quoted.

"*It was, then, clearly the design of Jesus Christ to*

put first in one alone, what afterwards He meant to put in several; but the sequence does not reverse the beginning, nor the first lose his place. That first word, ' Whatsoever thou shalt bind,' said to one alone has already ranged under his power each one of those to whom shall be said, ' Whatsoever ye shall remit;' for the promises of Jesus Christ, as well as His gifts, are without repentance; and what is once given indefinitely and universally is irrevocable : besides, that power given to several carries its restriction in its division, whilst power given to one alone, and over all, and without exception, carries with it plenitude, and, not having to be divided with any other, it has no bounds save those which its terms convey.

" Thus the mystery is understood : all receive the same power, and all from the same source; but not all in the same degree, nor with the same extent; for Jesus Christ communicates Himself in such measure as pleases Him, and always in the manner most suitable to establish the unity of His Church. This is why He begins with the first, and in that first He forms the whole, and Himself develops in order what He has put in one. ' And Peter,' says S. Augustine, 'who in the honour of his primacy represented the whole Church,'[1] receives also the first, and the only one at first, the keys which should afterwards be communicated to all the rest,[2] in order that we may learn, according to the doctrine of a holy Bishop of the Gallican

---

[1] S. Augustine.   [2] S. Optatus.

Church,[1] that the ecclesiastical authority, first established in the person of one alone, has only been diffused on the condition of being always brought back to the principle of its unity, and that all those who shall have to exercise it ought to hold themselves inseparably united to the same chair.

"This is that Roman chair so celebrated by the Fathers, which they have vied with each other in exalting as 'the chiefship of the Apostolic See;'[2] 'the superior chiefship;'[3] 'the source of unity;'[4] 'that most holy throne which has the headship over all the Churches of the world;'[5] 'the head of the Episcopate, the chiefship of the universal Church;'[6] 'the head of pastoral honour to the world;'[7] 'the head of the members;'[8] 'the single chair, in which all keep unity.'[9] In these words you hear S. Optatus, S. Augustine, S. Cyprian, S. Irenæus, S. Prosper, S. Avitus, S. Theodoret, the Council of Chalcedon, and the rest; Africa, Gaul, Greece, Asia, the East and the West together."[10]

Now, when S. Leo publicly in such an undoubting manner set forth from Holy Scripture itself the peculiar privileges of S. Peter's See, did he go

---

[1] Cæsarius of Arles to Pope Symmachus.

[2] S. August., *Ep.* 43.   [3] S. Irenæus, iii. 3.

[4] S. Cyp., *Ep.* 73.   [5] Theodoret, *Ep.* 116.

[6] S. Avitus, *ad Faust.*   [7] S. Prosper, *De Ingrat.*

[8] Council of Chalcedon to S. Leo.

[9] S. Optat., 2 *cont. Parm.*

[10] Bossuet, *Sermon sur l'Unité.*

beyond the minds of his hearers and the belief of
his age? So far from it, that the Eastern Church,
ever most jealous in this respect, assembled in a
council of more than six hundred Bishops, of which
two only, the Pope's own legates, were from the
West, of its own accord, and in the solemn act of a
synodal letter, addresses this very S. Leo in terms
equivalent to his own, which are even unintelligible
save upon the principles of S. Leo's discourse.[1]
They acknowledge him as sitting in the place of
Peter; "the interpreter to all of the voice of the
blessed Peter;" they declare that " he presided over
them as the head over the members;" they ask for his
consent to their acts, "because every success of the
children is reckoned to the parents who own it;"
they tell him that "he is intrusted by the Saviour
with the guardianship of the vine (ἀμπελου)," and
that, "shining himself in the full light of Apostolic
radiance, he had, with habitual regard, often extended this likewise to the Church of Constantinople, inasmuch as he could afford, without grudg-
ing, to impart his own blessings to his kindred;"
they pray him, as " they had introduced agreement
with the head in good things, so let the head fulfil
to the children what is fitting;" and finally they
say that the whole force of their acts will depend
on his confirmation.

I see not that the most vigorous defender of S.
Peter's rights has ever claimed for him greater
power than S. Leo exercised at the Council of

---

[1] Mansi, vi. 147-155.

Chalcedon, or greater than here, of its own accord, the Council attributes to him.

On the same basis of Holy Scripture the Council of Lateran, A.D. 1215, sets its decree : " The Roman Church, *by the disposition of the Lord*, holds the chiefship of ordinary power over all the rest, as being the mother and mistress of all the faithful of Christ." [1]

At the Council of Lyons, A.D. 1274, the Greeks were admitted to communion, confessing that " the holy Roman Church holds a supreme and full primacy and headship over the whole Catholic Church, which she truly and humbly acknowledges to have received from the Lord Himself, in the person of blessed Peter, the prince or head of the Apostles, whose successor is the Roman Pontiff, with plenitude of power." [2]

And the Council of Florence declares, that the holy Apostolic See and the Roman Pontiff hold a primacy over the whole world ; and that " the Roman Pontiff himself is successor of blessed Peter, prince of the Apostles, and true Vicar of Christ, and Head of the whole Church, and is Father and Doctor of all Christians ; and that to him, in the person of blessed Peter, full power was delivered by our Lord Jesus Christ to feed, to rule, and to govern the universal Church, as also is contained in the acts of Ecumenical Councils, and in the sacred canons." [3]

Surely the definition of these three later Councils,

[1] Mansi, xxii. 990.   [2] *Ibid*., xxiv. 71.
[3] *Ibid*., xxxi. 1031.

to which, in their day, the Church of England was bound, and from obedience to which I have never been able to learn in what way she has been delivered, asserts no more either than the words of our Lord Himself in the Holy Scripture, or than those of the Council of Chalcedon, in the middle of the fifth century, to which the Church of England still professes obedience.

Nor can I see how any honest mind can draw from our Lord's words and acts any other meaning than that set forth by S. Leo in the fifth century, and by Bossuet in the seventeenth century.

This, then, is the testimony of the Holy Scripture, and this the interpretation of the Church, respecting the Roman Primacy. If, through eighteen hundred years, two things alone have remained unshaken, the Christian Faith and the Apostolic See, perhaps it is because he who confessed, "Thou art the Christ, the Son of the living God," was forthwith made the Rock, against which every storm should strike in vain.

SECTION III.

THE END AND OFFICE OF THE PRIMACY.

" HOLY Father, keep through Thine own name
those whom Thou hast given Me, that they may be
one, as We are. . . . As Thou hast sent Me into
the world, even so have I also sent them into the
world. And for their sakes I sanctify Myself, that
they also may be sanctified through the truth.
Neither pray I for these alone, but for them also
which shall believe on Me through their word ;
that they all may be one, as Thou, Father, art in
Me and I in Thee, that they also may be one in
Us : that the world may believe that Thou hast
sent Me. And the glory which Thou gavest Me I
have given them ; that they may be one, even as
We are one : I in them, and Thou in Me, that they
may be made perfect in one ; and that the world
may know that Thou hast sent Me, and hast loved
them, as Thou hast loved Me." [1]

" The promises of Jesus Christ, as well as His
gifts, are without repentance ;" [2] and the prayers
of Jesus Christ are ever accomplished.

In this most sacred of all prayers, He tells us
the purpose of His mission into the world : " I have
finished the work which Thou gavest Me to do : "

---

[1] John xvii.   [2] Bousuet Sermon sur l'Unité.

and that work, to set up in the world, and out of
the world, but not of the world, an unity, of which
the model and prototype is, the unity of the Most
Holy Trinity: "that they all may be one, as Thou,
Father, art in Me and I in Thee, that they also
may be one in Us;" and a *visible unity*, for its
effect should be, "that the world may believe that
Thou hast sent Me."

Our Lord is praying for His Church, and in so
doing He sets it before us in its double unity,—
the unity of the Body, and the unity of the Spirit;
its unity as one visible society, and its unity as one
spiritual system : unities which may be in thought
distinguished and considered separately, but which
in fact involve each other, and are inseparable.
"There is one Body, and one Spirit," even as there
is "one Lord," who is in two natures, of which the
human has a body, and the divine is pure spirit;
and "one faith," in that same Christ, the Son of
the living God.

And now let us refer back the nature of each of
these unities to its great model and exemplar, the
Most Holy Trinity.

I. First, as to the unity of the Body.

What is that unity wherein the Father and the
Son are one? It is an unity of essence and of
origin. The Father is God, and the Son is God,
and yet there are not two Gods, because the Godhead of the Son is derived from the Father; nor
are there three, though the Holy Spirit is equally
God, because His Godhead proceeds from the same
fountain of Deity in the Father, through the Son.

What is the unity of the Church as a visible society—that one holy Catholic Church in which we all so often profess our belief? It is an unity of essence and of origin in its government, the one indivisible Episcopate. "Episcopatus unus, cujus a singulis in solidum pars tenetur."

Our Lord, in His prayer, deduces all from His own mission ; "as Thou hast *sent* Me into the world, even so have I also *sent* them into the world." The fountain of this visible unity, the root of this divine society, the source of all power to govern it, was in that divine Person to whom Peter said : " Thou art the Christ, the Son of the living God." Who by His answer communicated —for His promises, like His gifts, are without re-pentance—to the speaker that fountain, that root, and that power : " Thou art Peter, and upon this rock I will build My Church, and the gates of hell shall not prevail against it ; and I will give unto thee the keys of the kingdom of heaven." Here our Lord *marked out* one man as the head, after Himself, of that visible unity, which He had come into the world to set up. And when the work of redemption was complete, He *conferred* on that same man the power which He had here promised ; "Simon, son of Jonas, feed My sheep." So S. Augustine, inheriting the doctrine of S. Cyprian, tells us : " He saith to Peter, *in whose single person He casts the mould of His Church :* Peter, lovest thou Me?"[1]

----

[1] Serm. cxlvii., c. 2.

Our Lord, throughout His Gospel, calls that one visible society a kingdom,—this is he to whom He gave its keys ; and one fold,—this is its shepherd ; and a family,—this is the elder brother to whom He said : " Confirm thy brethren ; " and a household,—this is " the faithful and wise steward," whom the Lord hath made ruler over it ; Solomon calls it an army,—this is its general ; and S. Paul a body,—this is, after Christ, its head.

For it was to remain, from the Lord's first coming to His second, a kingdom, a fold, a family, a household, an army, and a body; all which are visible unities. How, then, should it not have a visible head to all these ? How should not he, to whom the Lord departing said, " Feed My sheep," continue in the person of his successors to feed them for ever, till the great Shepherd should appear at His manifestation ?

This is what General Councils have exclaimed : " Peter hath spoken by Leo,"[1] " Peter hath spoken by Agatho." This is what the whole line of Saints has believed, and in this faith has lived and died : " Blessed Peter, who in his own see lives and rules, grants to those who seek it the truth of the faith."[2]

What is that which makes a kingdom one ?— the derivation of all jurisdiction from its sovereign ; or an army one ?—the concentration of all authority in its general ; or a household one, but the rule of its master ? or a body one, but the perpetual influence of its head ? or what unites the countless

[1] The Council of Chalcedon, and the Sixth Council, in 680.
[2] S. Peter Chrysologus to the heretic Eutyches.

sheep of the visible Church in one fold here on earth, but the one shepherd, who represents the Lord?

Two sovereigns, two generals with supreme power, two masters, two heads, two shepherds, destroy altogether the idea of these respective unities.

But our Lord takes us higher than these. He prays that "they may be one, as We are." Now two or more sources of deity would make two or more gods. So two or more sources of power in His Church, viewed as a visible society, would make two or more Churches. But He willed that Church to be one for ever, and He made it one by the unity of source in its perpetual government. He set up one indivisible Episcopate, which had not its like in things of earth, and found its exemplar only in the divine essence; in that unity of three Persons which consists in having one source of deity.

The ancient Saint, who speaks of "one Episcopate, a part of which is held by each without division of the whole," is in that same place setting forth precisely this unity of the Church, as springing from one source. He asks why men are deceived; and he answers, because "they do not return to *the origin of truth*, nor *seek the head*." In that case there "would not be need of arguments." What is this origin? who this head? he goes on. The Lord says to Peter: "Thou art Peter," etc. On his single person He builds His Church. This person of Peter he points out as the source of many rays, the root of a tree spreading into many branches, the fountain-head of countless streams fertilising the earth. Yet in all these, "unity is preserved in the origin." It is evident that so long as the unity abides, the origin must abide too ; he is contemplating an ever-springing source of an ever-living power. And he then refers to the Holy Trinity as the type of this : "The Lord says : I and the Father are one. And, again, of the Father, and the Son, and the Holy Spirit, it is written : And these three are one. And does anybody believe that this unity, coming from the divine solidity, cohering by means of heavenly sacraments, *can possibly* be divided in the Church, and divorced by the collision of wills ? " So Pope Symmachus (A.D. 500) says : " After the manner of the Trinity whose power is one and indivisible, there is one Episcopate in diverse prelates."[1] God the Father is the source of this power in the Godhead, and S. Peter's chair of this unity in the Episcopate. S. Cyprian and S. Symmachus are equally setting forth this prayer of our Lord.

Let the Church be extended to any degree in the number of her Bishops, yet she is one, and they are one, in "the unity of origin ;" not merely in that Peter *was* one "from whom the very Episcopate and all the authority of this title sprung ;"[2] but in that Peter *is* still one, and that now, in the nineteenth century, just as when S. Leo said it in the fifth : " If anything, even in our time, by us

[1] Mansi, tom. viii. 208 b.
[2] S. Innocent to the Council of Milevi.

be rightly done and rightly ordered, it is to be
ascribed to his working, to his guidance, unto whom
it was said : 'And thou, when thou art converted,
confirm thy brethren ;' and to whom the Lord,
after His resurrection, in answer to the triple profession of eternal love, thrice said with mystical
intent : ' Feed My sheep.'' And this, beyond a
doubt, the pious shepherd does even now, and
fulfils the charge of his Lord."

In truth, we are living men, with living souls,
and we need a living Church, and not a dead one.
Those who can bear that the Body of Christ should
be corrupt, may also endure that it once was alive,
but is now dead ; or that it once was one, but is
now three.   All these three notions can indeed
only be expressed by an honest word which arose
in a dishonest time ;—they are a *sham*, and they
who put them forward do not at the bottom believe
either in the one Body or in the one Spirit ; for it
is evident that the one Body perishes when the one
Spirit ceases to animate it.   What will it help the
wandering soul to tell it, there was once a teacher
sent from God, but he had ceased to bear God's
commission ?   Or the wrecked mariner, there was
once a ship, which rode the waves bravely, but it
is not now within your reach?   And what will it
help one who is longing, aching, perishing, for the
truth, to answer, there once was a Church, "the
pillar and ground of the truth," and so it remained,
as long as it was undivided, that is, for many
hundred years ; but it *is* divided now, and therefore is now no longer the pillar and ground of the

truth; but stay where you are, and hold all which that Church held, and you will be safe?

This is Anglicanism.

Was it for this that our Lord prayed, "that they all may be one, as Thou, Father, art in Me, and I in Thee, that they also may be one in Us : that the world may believe that Thou hast sent Me?"

Or does S. Peter still sit in his one chair? Is he still the living source of a living Episcopate? Does he still proclaim, with the voice of the one universal Church : "Thou art the Christ, the Son of the living God?" Does he still hear in answer : "Thou art Peter, and upon this rock I will build My Church, and the gates of hell shall not prevail against it?"

This is Catholicism.

"Peter," says S. Augustine, "represented the very universality and unity of the Church."[1] And this Episcopate, which has its living source in the person of Peter's successor, and its centre in his chair, which is thus derived from him, and perpetually carried back to him, can and does embrace the whole earth, extends unto all nations, for no difference of race or speech is "foreign" to the household of saints, makes all languages one, for it has the Pentecostal gift, and this is surely universality; and yet is gathered up, directed, influenced, held together, by one, a Bishop himself, and having a particular flock, a Bishop of Bishops, and having an universal one, and this is surely

---

[1] *Serm.* ccxcv.

unity.   The whole Episcopate is mortised into
that rock of Peter, by which it is one and immovable.   Separate a portion of it from that rock,
and it is no longer "one Episcopate, a part of
which is held by each *without division of the whole.*"
That division mars all.   With unity strength, and
with strength courage, departs, and the spring of
its power is gone ; it no longer stands in one place ;
its footing is lost; the powers of the world set their
feet on its neck ; and for that one voice, " Thou
art Christ, the Son of the living God," which is the
voice of the Rock, it is much if. it do not cry when
the world accuses it, " I know not the man." To
" One Body and one Spirit, one Lord and one
Faith," what is added ?—" One Baptism." And
by those who do not stand on Peter's Rock this
one Baptism for the remission of sins will be declared a difficult and mysterious doctrine, understood by pious minds in different ways, and therefore not to be imposed on any.   To make God's
truth an open question is to deny the Lord when
you are accused of being His disciple.

But impart that one and true Episcopate to as
many as you will, its voice will be one and its
power one, its rule equal, its courage unswerving,
because the "unity of its origin " is one, and "the
Catholic Church throughout all the world will be
one bridal chamber of Christ." [1]

The end and office of the Primacy, therefore, in
respect to the Church as a visible society, is the

---

[1] Decree of Pope Gelasius and seventy Bishops, A.D. 494, de-
termining the Canon of Scripture.   Mansi, viii. 147.

maintenance of unity, which is upheld now and through all time, and in all countries, as it was in the upper chamber of Jerusalem, because the source of its organisation is one.

II. But this unity is itself subservient to a higher one: that most sacred Body of the Lord, beside His reasonable Soul, is inhabited by the eternal Spirit of His Godhead; and this, His mystical Body, has too its Spirit,—the Spirit of truth, leading it into all truth. This outward framework has a system of divine teaching committed to it, a perpetual deposit. Of this too the Lord said: "The glory which Thou gavest Me I have given them; that they may be one, even as We are one: I in them, and Thou in Me, that they may be made perfect in one, and that the world may know that Thou hast sent Me." How are the Father and the Son one?—By the Holy Spirit, which is their love. How is the Church one?—By that Holy Spirit dwelling in her. How is the voice of that Spirit made known?—By that same organ of visible unity; by that Rock which cries, "Thou art Christ, the Son of the living God:" by him who perpetually confirms his brethren; by him who is charged that he love more than all, because he has the charge of the whole flock. Peter calls his brethren together, Peter asks their counsel, Peter collects their suffrages, Peter confirms their voice. In so doing, he represents their universality; or, again, as the one chief shepherd, as the one keeper of the door and holder of the keys, as having in himself the power to bind and to loose all, even

the whole number of his brethren, whether collected, or distributed in their several pastures, he
pronounces himself, and in so doing he represents
their unity. United with a general council, he
shows to the world that the Church is universal;
from his own watch-tower, the loftiest of all, he
proclaims to that same world that she is one.[1]

Where Peter speaks, you have one faith, one
homogeneous and harmonious system of teaching
—sacraments which embrace the whole spiritual
life from the cradle to the grave. He teaches that
infants are received into God's kingdom by the
laver of regeneration in Baptism, nor are his
disciples shocked at his voice; because he likewise
teaches them, that if those who have received this
divine gift sin, they can only recover it by penance:
they must enter afresh into that kingdom out of
which they have wantonly cast themselves, by the
second baptism of tears, and the plank which remains for the shipwrecked : where Peter's voice is
not heard, the doctrine of Baptism is either taught
without the doctrine of penance, and then it be-
comes at once a stumbling-block, or it is not
taught at all, and the whole sacramental system is
overthrown. He teaches, moreover, that our Lord
has established a real ministry for the forgiveness
of sins, and bestowed on men a real power to consecrate His Body, the source of unspeakable blessings to men, the inexhaustible fountain of
sanctity, the spring of superhuman love. This it

---

[1] This thought is from De Maistre; I forget the reference.

is which enables him to ask of those who listen to his teaching the surrender of their dearest affections, and the life of angels upon earth. And he teaches this, not in an ambiguous, hesitating manner, as one rather ashamed of his message, who would rather insinuate than state what he had to say ; but he is plain-spoken in his premises, bold and consistent in his deductions.

From the Divinity of our Lord's Person he infers that the Lord's Mother has an office and a function in His kingdom of love : from the reality of His Eucharistic Presence He proclaims that Saints live and reign with Him, hear prayers, and work miracles. The world listens, and sneers, and cavils, and disbelieves, is affronted, abuses, persecutes ; but the elect are converted and saved.

Go to those who once acknowledged Peter as their Doctor and Teacher, who left him in possession of his full inheritance, and you will find this consistent and harmonious system mainly held indeed, but somehow afflicted with sterility, a "Church in petrifaction," as some one has called it.

Go to those who left Peter denouncing him as a corrupter of God's truth, as Antichrist sitting in Christ's seat, and you find this divine system broken into fragments : some holding one part, and some another, all exaggerating what they have, and depreciating what they have not, and misunderstanding the whole. There is no longer any agreement, no longer the shadow of one faith. The dissentients broke into numberless bodies, and have been breaking off more and more ever since :

they set out with acknowledging an authority,
which they put in themselves, but they finish with
denying that there is any, and proclaiming as
their indefeasible right the liberty to judge Scripture for themselves, and to deduce from it what
seems good to such private judgment : a corollary
to which in a tolerant and luxurious age like our
own, is this, that every one has indeed a right to
his own opinion, but that no one should impose
such opinion on his neighbour ; and thus all truth
is got rid of.

Or if there be one part of those dissentients in
whom from the beginning there was more worldly
policy than sincerity of belief, however erroneous ;
if there was one province of Christ's mystical
kingdom, on which Cæsar had cast longing eyes,
and said in his heart : " Give me but the sceptre of
Christ, and I shall be omnipotent : " think you that
worldly law and Cæsar's policy have had power to
arrest the downward descent, to maintain the one
inheritance of faith, to set it forth in its simplicity
and purity ? Alas ! what do you find ?—ambiguous
formularies, studiously so drawn up to be signed in
different senses by those who minister at the same
altar : a system so ill compacted that those who
believe in sacraments are tormented by one half
which they engage to maintain, and those who dis-
believe them have to drug their consciences as to
the other half ; and these two parties, opposed in
every principle of their belief, this bundle of Luthero-
Calvinist heresies stifling Catholic truths, held
together by a civil law, and by the anxiety of a

State,—which has no conscience of its own, and looks on all dogma with sheer indifference,—to wield a weapon of great influence, a system based on worldly comfort and outward respectability, instead of the pure unearthly aims, the keen faith, and self-denying life of the one Bride of Christ.

Can this be that of which our Lord spake?— " that they all may be one, as Thou, Father, art in Me and I in Thee, that they also may be one in Us : that the world may believe that Thou hast sent Me."

What, on the other hand, is the belief which has been from the first at the very heart of the Church, which has inspirited her members from age to age to stand against the world, to disregard its frowns, to think a life well spent in maintaining a point of doctrine, and death endured in behalf of any part of her teaching, a martyrdom? What else but that there is one faith lodged within her, which it is her very function to guard, set forth, and apply, to unfold from the germ to the full and perfect fruit, to draw from the pregnant sentences and short intimations of Holy Writ, to harmonise and arrange, distribute and portion out, so that man, woman, and child, may find in it their stay, that Saints may grow up under its nurture, and its fruit be for the healing of the nations? And, what is part and parcel of this belief, that as our Lord's presence was with Peter and his brethren, in those first days, and throughout their ministry, so it would be evermore. The Comforter, whom He had promised, was not to be given for one generation, or one century, or two or four, and then to be withdrawn, but for ever. He could not fail the body in which He dwelt, while Peter presided over it in person; as little could He fail, in the fifth century, when one of Peter's successors presided in his place; as little in the ninth, or the twelfth, or the fifteenth; as little in the nineteenth, or in any to come. *For to suppose His failing is to ignore the whole idea on which the Church is built:* it is to turn the mystical body of Christ into a school of philosophy, a branch of learning. Had it been so, the Lower Empire would have corrupted it, the Barbarians have swept it away with sword and flame, the Reformation have torn it to pieces, and Voltaire laughed it out of the world.

Not a Council which ever sat, not a Father who ever wrote, not a martyr who ever suffered, but believed in a perpetual illuminating grace of the Holy Spirit dwelling in the Church of God to the end of time. Without it Councils and Fathers would not have existed, and still less martyrs. Men do not suffer for *opinions*, but for faith. And now, as age after age went on, as the Church burst the limits of the Roman Empire, and added nation after nation to her sway, as she passed the Atlantic and the Indian Ocean, what power within her was to hold together that wide system of teaching worked out into such manifold detail? What power to eject from her bosom heresy after heresy, which by the will of God was to arise and try her, winnow the wheat, and scatter the chaff? That same power which guarded and maintained the unity and universality of her outward framework became the voice of the Holy Spirit within her, defining and ordering her faith. Her Episcopate did not break into fragments within each separate nation, and constitute systems of government coextensive with their several sovereignties, because the perpetual fountain of the one Episcopate had its spring and plenitude in S. Peter's See, and every individual who held a part of it held it *without division of the whole:* and her faith remained one, homogeneous, and complete, because it was the faith of Peter, which could not fail, because the one Shepherd led the whole flock into the same pastures, because as Peter had spoken by Leo and spoken by Agatho, so likewise he spoke by Innocent and by Pius; so he gathers the voices of his brethren now lifted from eight hundred provinces to one throne, weighs them in his wisdom, and gives them a single expression and an universal potency. He who breaks from the Body of the Universal Pastor commits schism; he who disregards the voice of the Universal Pastor falls into heresy. S. Celestine judged Nestorius, and S. Leo judged Eutyches; and their heresies were cast out of the Church, and carried with them the whole sacramental system of the Church, and an indisputable Episcopal Succession; they laid hold of nations, and lasted for centuries; their heresies might seem to men of the world subtle metaphysical misconceptions. I doubt not that six of the most learned lawyers, of the most unimpeachable integrity, which England could produce, would pronounce that both were "open questions," and might be innocently held ; and that men's " consciences must be set on hair-triggers," to fight about such things.   But nevertheless two Popes judged those heresies, and God has judged them too ; their prestige is past away ; no civil power finds it worth while any longer to live upon them.   But the Church of God goes on still upon her course; the voice of Peter still lives within her. She is still one in her outward framework, one in her inward belief; she still claims to be obeyed and trusted, because the See of Peter is within her, and the presence which cannot fail, the power which enunciates truths, and makes saints, has its organ in that voice, and abides by that rock.

SECTION IV.

THE POWER OF THE PRIMACY.

WE have seen that the *end* for which our Lord instituted the Primacy was the maintenance of unity in His mystical Body, its twofold unity of a great visible society, and a great spiritual system of belief; in other words, of communion, and of faith. From His own divine Person as the God-Man, the visible society, and the faith which animates it, sprang ; and He established unity both in the one and in the other for ever, by appointing one from age to age to represent that Person, and in that capacity to be the ever-springing source of all power to govern the society, the ever-living voice which gives expression to its belief.

The man so selected was S. Peter ; and what S. Peter was in the Apostolic Body, every successor of his has been, is, and shall be to the end of time in the " One Episcopate, in which a part is held by each *without division of the whole.*"

The *end* for which the Primacy was instituted guides us, then, to the nature of its *power*, which is, a jurisdiction universal, immediate, and supreme.

How was this conveyed ? In a manner quite in

accordance with other acts of our Lord and with His teaching.

Is He not wont to gather up all His dispensations in a few words of profound depth and meaning, which perhaps it will require ages to develop? What are His parables but so many pictures, which convey to us, each without crowding, and in space incredibly small, the nature of His kingdom, the working of His grace, the fortunes of His Church?

It would seem as if He delighted to repeat in language, the poor vehicle of human thought, the miracles which He works in nature, when He paints on the retina of the eye a boundless and varied landscape, every object in its due proportion, every colour and form preserved, on a point of space so minute.

In the most ancient of all prophecies He summed up the whole of His revelation to man, all that He Himself was to do, and much that yet remains to be unfolded, at "the restitution of all things," when He declared that the Seed of the woman should bruise the serpent's head.   All subsequent prophecy was but the unfolding of this.

So in the creation of His mystical Body He set forth in a word the person of its ruler, and the nature of its perpetual government.

He spoke to Peter *once in promise:* " Thou art Peter, and upon this rock I will build My Church and the gates of hell shall not prevail against it; and I will give unto thee the keys of the kingdom of heaven."

And *once in performance:* "Feed My lambs: be shepherd over My sheep: feed My sheep."

It was the voice of the Creator, summing up His work in a word, for hence the whole organisation of His Church has sprung.   Age after age was to bring to light more and more the force of these words.   Time has not yet exhausted the first prophecy, nor has it told us all which is contained in His words to Peter.

But thus from the first the Primacy *contained* the Episcopate ; and the privileges of Metropolitans, Primates, and Patriarchs, are but emanations from the fountain-head, which sends forth larger or lesser streams as the case may require, but remains itself full.

The Priest is the centre of unity, both as to communion and faith, in his parish ; the Bishop in his diocese ; but he who heard " Feed My sheep," in the whole Episcopate ; which he represents and carries in his person, which sprung forth originally from that person, and is now maintained in it.

Is this a new belief?   Nay, it is the doctrine of all antiquity, the *only* view which ancient saints give us of the government of Christ's Church ; the only view which will give connection and harmony to the facts of ecclesiastical history.

This is what S. Cyprian meant when he called S. Peter's chair " the root and womb of the Catholic Church." [1]

Or let us take the public letters of the most

[1] *Ep. 45 to Pope Cornelius.*

ancient Popes which have come down to us,—documents incomparably more authoritative than the words of any particular Father, because, though signed by the Pope alone, they were the acts of his Council likewise, transmitted to Primates of provinces, by them to be communicated to Bishops, and received as having the force of laws.

Pope Boniface I., A.D. 422, to whom S. Augustine dedicated one of his works, thus writes to the Bishops of Thessaly :

"*The formation of the Universal Church at its birth took its beginning from the honour of blessed Peter, in whose person its regimen and sum consists. For from his fountain the stream ·of ecclesiastical discipline flowed forth into all Churches, as the culture of religion progressively advanced.* The precepts of the Nicene Council bear witness to nothing else : so that it ventured not to appoint anything over him, seeing that nothing could possibly be conferred above his deserts : moreover, *it knew that everything had been granted to him by the word of the Lord.* `Certain, therefore, is it that this Church is to the Churches diffused throughout the whole world, as it were, the head of its own members ; from which whosoever cuts himself off, becomes expelled from the Christian religion, as he has begun not to be in the one compact structure* (compages).[1]

" For this purpose the Apostolic See holds the headship, that it may receive the lawful complaints of all."

---

[1] Coustant., *Ep. Rom. Pontific.*, p. 1037.

At the beginning of the fifth century, the Pope speaks of what was ancient, recognised and indisputable, based on the words of Holy Writ, and acknowledged by the first great General Council.

Let us take another passage, which points out the difference between Order and Jurisdiction in the members of the Apostolic College itself, and so in the Episcopal Body since ; for, on the right understanding of this distinction, and of the consequences which flow from it, depends the understanding of the whole constitution of the Church as a visible society ; and a misconception, an incoherence here, will confuse the whole vision, and make a man, with the best intentions, unable to locate, or estimate, the strongest proofs brought before him.

S. Leo was deriving a part of his own universal Primacy to the Bishop of Thessalonica ; that is, he was giving him, over and above his proper powers as Bishop of the individual see of Thessalonica, a power to represent the Pope, constituting him, in fact, a Patriarch over the ten Metropolitans of eastern Illyricum, including Greece ; just as the Bishop of Alexandria was over Egypt, and the Bishop of Antioch over the East, that is, the province called Oriens.   These are S. Leo's own words : " As my predecessors to your predecessors, so have I, following the example of those gone before, *committed to your affection my charge of government ;* that you, imitating our gentleness, *might relieve the care, which we, in virtue of our headship, by divine institution, owe to all Churches,* and might in some degree discharge our personal visitation to provinces far distant from us. . . . . For we have intrusted your affection to represent us on this condition, *that you are called to a part of our solicitude, but not to the fulness of our power.* . . . . But if, in a matter which you believe fit to be considered and decided on with your brethren, their sentence differs from yours, let everything be referred to us on the authority of the Acts, that all doubtfulness may be removed, and we may decree what pleaseth God. . . . . *For the compactness of our unity cannot remain firm, unless the bond of charity weld us into an insepar- able whole;* because, ' as we have many members in one Body, and all members have not the same office, so we, being many, are one Body in Christ, and every one members one of another.' For it is the connection of the whole body which makes one soundness and one beauty ; and this connection, as it requires unanimity in the whole body, so especi- ally demands concord among Bishops. For, *though these have a like dignity, yet have they not an equal jurisdiction : since even among the most blessed Apostles, as there was a likeness of honour, so was there a certain distinction of power ; and, the election of all being equal, pre-eminence over the rest was given to one. From which type the distinction also between Bishops has arisen,* and it was provided by a great ordering, that all should not claim to them- selves all things, but that in every province there should be one, whose sentence should be considered the first among his brethren; and others again, seated in the greater cities, should undertake a larger care, *through whom the direction of the Universal Church should converge to the one See of Peter, and nothing anywhere disagree from its head.*"

S. Leo wrote this five years before the fourth General Council, which called him, as we have seen, " head over the members," and " father of the children," and " intrusted with the care of the vine by the Saviour." It is impossible for expressions more perfectly to tally than those of the Council with those of the Pope.

Let us consider what S. Leo tells us here.

First, he observes that while the Apostles were equal as to all power of Order, that is, as to the whole Sacerdotium, as to what is conferred by consecration, yet as to how they should exercise this power, in what places, and under what conditions, they were put under one, *viz.* S. Peter. And thus, even though they were sent into all the world by our Lord Himself, yet that mission was to be exercised under the pre-eminence of one. This means, in other words, that S. Peter's superiority consisted in his jurisdiction over them, exactly as S. Jerome says: "Among the twelve one is chosen out, that by the appointment of a head the opportunity for schism might be taken away."

Secondly, " from this type the distinction between Bishops has arisen," namely, that while all were equal as to the Sacerdotium (as the same S Jerome says, " wherever a Bishop is, be it at Rome,

or Eugubium, or Constantinople, or Rhegium, or
Alexandria, or Tanæ, he is of the same *rank*, the
same *priesthood*"), the jurisdiction of one differs in
extent from that of another, as is self-evident in
the cases of Rome, and Constantinople, and Alexandria: but likewise, to complete the type, there is
a jurisdiction extending equally over all; there is
one Peter among the Apostles, and there is Peter's
successor too among the Bishops. This he goes on
to say. For,—

Thirdly, There is the Bishop over the Diocese,
the Metropolitan over the Province, the Primate,
or Patriarch, over the Patriarchate,—but all this
for one end,—" in which the regimen and sum," as
Pope Boniface observes, " consists,"—namely, that
" *through* them the direction of the Universal
Church should converge to the one See of Peter,
and nothing anywhere disagree from its head."

Now here, in the Apostolic, and in the Episcopal
Body, in the original " Forma," and in the " Com-
pages" which sprung from it, there are two powers,
and no more, of divine institution :—the Primacy
of Peter, and the co-Episcopate of the Apostles ;
the Primacy of Peter's successor, and the co-Episcopate of his brethren.

All that is between, Metropolitical, Primatial, or
Patriarchal arrangements, are only of ecclesiastical
growth, and therefore subject to diminution, or increase, or alteration ; they do but " relieve the care
which, in virtue of his headship, by divine institution, the Universal Primate owes to all Churches."
The power of this Primate suffers no diminution

from their existence; they are not set up *against* him, but *under* him; not to *withdraw* "the care which, in virtue of his headship, he owes to all Churches," but to "*relieve* it."

Circumstances may make it expedient that under him metropolitical powers should be concentrated for whole provinces in single hands, which should accordingly confirm their subject Bishops, or even Archbishops.

Circumstances again may make it expedient that the Universal Primate should directly and immediately give institution to all Bishops.

But in the one case, equally as in the other, he is *supreme.* If the Patriarch is accused, he hears, judges, absolves, or condemns him. If his ordination is objected to, he confirms or annuls it; if his faith is doubted, he clears or he deprives him. If he is tyrannical, his subject Bishops appeal to the One Head, and are righted. .

In the earliest times, when near three centuries of persecution were to try the rising Church, it was expedient, for various reasons, that powers belonging in their fulness to the universal Primate should be imparted, in a large degree, to others under him : yet, to mark plainly the *source* of these powers, in both cases the missions proceeded from S. Peter. To Alexandria, the second city of the Roman empire, he sent his disciple Mark, with patriarchal powers ; at Antioch, the third city, he had sat himself for seven years, and with it he left a portion of his pre-eminence. But the fulness and supremacy of that power which his Lord had given to him,

for the unity of the mystical Body, he deposited at
Rome. In the first four centuries no See possessed
patriarchal powers but the three Sees of Peter.
Why did no Apostle leave his Apostolic jurisdiction to any Church? S. Paul had founded
Ephesus, and S. John had exercised his Apostolic
power over it, and all the province of Asia, after
Peter's death, but the Bishop of Ephesus held only
an inferior rank. Constantinople rose to patriarchal
rank only by the overbearing domination of the
Greek Emperors, and Jerusalem out of respect to
the Lord's city in the fifth century.

The intense jealousy of everything Western,
which is apparent in the Greek mind from the
beginning, and after many minor schisms burst out
into fatal violence in the time of Photius, is another
reason why great powers were given to the Sees
of Alexandria and Antioch in the first ages.

But if the Pope, in the " greater causes," called
them to account, his supremacy is undoubted.

In later times it has been thought expedient that
powers, which at their commencement were emanations from S. Peter's Primacy, as we have seen in
the case of Thessalonica, should return to his See,
and that the Head of the whole body should
directly " confirm his brethren."

Many reasons, doubtless, there were for this,—
for instance, would not the very strong nationality
which characterises modern times have broken up
the Church into fragments, had the chief Bishop
of each nation possessed patriarchal powers, whereas the strong arm of the Roman empire had

moulded into one many opposite races, though it could not overcome the inherent antagonism of the Greek to the Latin? Would not, again, the violent jealousy of the civil power have forced its own subjects in each nation to surrender the free exercise of their spiritual rights, but for that bond of divine institution by which our Lord fastened them to the See of S. Peter? Alas for the hapless Church which has broken that bond! Statesmen without a creed will ride over it rough-shod, and lawyers decide points of faith, having power to agonise the conscience, as " in case of appeal from the Admiral's Court."

Thus in the middle of the fifth century the universal supremacy of S. Peter's See, as to the government of the Church's visible society, was publicly stated, both by Pope and by General Council, and lies at the basis of the whole structure of the Church's discipline in the preceding centuries. In its essence it was exactly the same, in its extent neither more nor less than it is now: for it was given by our Lord at the birth of the Church, and all other and inferior powers were sealed up in it.

But was this supremacy equally indisputable in matters of faith? Here we might answer, that he who is the source of jurisdiction *must* likewise be the supreme judge of doctrine : for the one great and visible society lives by and on its faith, and he who maintains unity in its outward framework must likewise guard that belief, and preserve pure the soul which animates the body. Moreover, so often as outward communion is imperilled by a breach of faith, the question of faith is inextricably mixed up with the question of communion, and one decision determines both. The claim of spiritual jurisdiction will crush any power, save that which Christ has made to bear it. Or, again, we might say that, as a fact, we owe the true doctrine of the Incarnation, under God, to this same S. Leo. The Eastern Church, partly overborne by the civil power, whose chief minister was a friend of the heresiarch, and partly sick of a deep inward taint which it never had strength to throw off, had gone into the heresy of Eutyches; legitimately assembled in a General Council, it had actually accepted his doctrine. S. Leo annulled the Council; S. Leo condemned the doctrine. He caused to assemble once more in a larger Council that East which through centuries was swayed backward and forward by the will of its princes, caused six hundred Bishops to receive his letter, word for word, in which the true faith was authoritatively defined, and so was the means of keeping them for four centuries, as it were in spite of themselves, in the unity of the Church.

But we will turn to another controversy—one of the most subtle which has ever distressed the Church —one which harassed S. Augustine for many a year. Whither, after all his labours, writings, and prayers, in the Pelagian controversy, did he turn for its final solution? To S. Peter's chair. Two African Councils had condemned Pelagius, and their decrees, drawn up by S. Augustine, were sent for approval to Pope Innocent I., together with

another letter from S. Augustine himself and some
friends, in which he says : "We do not pour back
our *streamlet* for the purpose of increasing your great
fountain, but in this, not however a slight temptation of the time (whence may He deliver us, to
whom we cry, Lead us not into temptation!), we
wish it to be decided by you *whether our stream,
however small, flows forth from that same head of
rivers whence comes your own abundance;* and by
your answers to be consoled respecting our common
participation of one grace." [1]

In reply, A.D. 416, S. Innocent praises the Council
of Carthage, that "in inquiring concerning these
matters, which it behoves to be treated with all
care by Bishops, and especially by a true, just, and
Catholic Council, observing the precedents of ancient
tradition, and mindful of ecclesiastical discipline,
you have confirmed the strength of our religion not
less now in consulting us, than by sound reason
before you pronounced sentence, inasmuch as you
approved of reference being made to our judgment,
knowing what is due to the Apostolic See, since all
we who are placed in this position desire to follow
the Apostle himself, *from whom the very Episcopate and all the authority of this title sprung.*
Following whom we know as well how to condemn
the evil as to approve the good. And this too,
that, guarding, according to the duty of Bishops,
the institutions of the Fathers, ye resolve that these
regulations should not be trodden under foot, which

[1] *Epist.*, p. 177.

they, *in pursuance of no human but a Divine sentence, have decreed ; viz., that whatever was being carried on, although in the most distant and remote provinces, should not be terminated before it was brought to the knowledge of this See ; by the full authority of which the just sentence should be confirmed, and that thence all other Churches might derive what they should order, whom they should absolve, whom, as being bemired with ineffaceable pollution, the stream that is worthy only of pure bodies should avoid ; so that from their parent source all waters should flow, and through the different regions of the whole world the pure streams of the fountain well forth uncorrupted."* [1]

Here we have S. Innocent affirming, (1) that questions respecting the Faith had always been referred to the judgment of the Holy See : (2) that this tradition rested on Scripture, that is on the prerogatives granted by our Saviour to S. Peter: (3) that decisions emanating from the Holy See were not liable to any error, " that the pure streams of the fountain should well forth uncorrupted : " (4) that all the Churches of the world had ever been bound to conform to them, " that thence all other Churches might derive what they should order," etc.[2]

To the Council of Numidia S. Innocent says : " Therefore do ye diligently and becomingly consult the secrets of the Apostolical honour (that honour, I mean, on which, beside those things that are without, the care of all the Churches attends), as to what judgment is to be passed on doubtful

[1] Coustant., *Ep. Rom. Pontif.*, p. 868.
[2] Petit Didier, *in loc.*

matters, following, in sooth, the prescription of the ancient rule, which you know, as well as I, has ever been preserved in the whole world. But this I pass by, for I am sure your prudence is aware of it : for how could you by your actions have confirmed this, save as knowing that throughout all provinces answers are ever emanating as from the Apostolic fountain to inquirers ? Especially so often as a matter of faith is under discussion, I conceive that all our brethren and fellow-Bishops can only refer to Peter, that is, *the source of their own name and honour*, just as your affection hath now referred, for what may benefit all Churches in common throughout the whole world. For the inventors of evils must necessarily become more cautious, when they see that at the reference of a double synod they have been severed from Ecclesiastical Communion by our sentence. Therefore your charity will enjoy a double advantage ; for you will have at once the satisfaction of having observed the canons, and the whole world will have the use of what you have gained : for who among Catholics will choose any longer to hold discourse with the adversaries of Christ ? "

Here we may observe, besides what was said above, (1) that nothing concerning faith was held for decided, before it was carried to the See of S. Peter, and had received the Pope's sentence : (2) that before his sentence the determination of particular Councils only held good provisionally,— " what judgment is to be passed on doubtful matters :" (3) that such determination only had the force of a consultation or relation as to a difficulty, made to the Pope before his own sentence,—" at the relation," he says, "of a double synod :" (4) that the Pope's sentence, by which he confirmed Councils, was a final judgment, excluding the condemned from the Church's Communion, "when they see that they have been severed from Ecclesiastical Communion by our sentence :" (5) that Bishops, as well as the faithful in general, always submitted themselves to such a decree. " Who among Catholics will choose any longer to hold discourse with the adversaries of Christ ? " [1]

S. Innocent the Third could have said no more about the powers of his See : what does S. Augustine observe upon it ?

" He answered to all as was right, and as it became the prelate of the Apostolical See." [2]   And as to the effect of his answer, there are famous words of S. Augustine, which have passed into a proverb : " Already two Councils on this matter have been sent to the Apostolic See ; replies from whence have also been received.   *The cause is terminated;* would that the error may presently terminate likewise ! " [3]

We need no more to tell us what S. Augustine meant by that " Headship, which," he says, "had ever flourished in the Apostolic See." [4]   It involves, we see, the necessity that all other Churches should agree in faith with it, as having deposited in itself the root of the Apostolic confession, concerning the

---

[1] Petit Didier, *in loc.*   [2] *Epist.* 186.
[3] Tom. v. p. 645, *Serm.* cxxxi.   [4] *Epist.* 43.

two natures of our Lord, to which the promise was given by our Lord, that the Church should be built upon it. S. Augustine and S. Innocent express the one true faith under S. Cyprian's image of the fountain, who in the same most remarkable passage where he sets forth the "one Episcopate, of which each holds a part without division of the whole," says, "as from one fountain numberless rivers flow, widely as their number may be diffused in broad abundance, yet unity is preserved in the source ;—one still is the head, and the origin one."

The power, therefore, which was to maintain unity of faith and of communion, does so, and can only do so, by having, both in matters concerning faith and in those concerning communion, a coactive jurisdiction, universal, immediate, and supreme. And in the fifth century this power is seen in undisputed operation, referring back to our Lord's institution as its source, and to all preceding ages of the Church for its exercise, and no one charges it with usurpation. And here I must go forward a thousand years, to the date of the Council of Constance, for the purpose of quoting one who was the soul of that Council, and the originator of what are called Gallican opinions, who yet, as will be seen, expresses exactly the same doctrine as S. Innocent and S. Leo above, respecting the relation between the Papacy and the Episcopate.

"The Papal dignity was instituted by Christ, supernaturally and immediately, as holding a monarchical and royal primacy in the ecclesiastical hierarchy, according to which unique and supreme

dignity the Church militant is called one under
Christ: which dignity whosoever presumes to im-
pugn or diminish, or reduce to the level of any
particular dignity, if he does this obstinately, is a
heretic, a schismatic, impious and sacrilegious. For
he falls into a heresy so often expressly condemned
from the very beginning of the Church to this day,
as well by Christ's institution of the headship of
Peter over the other Apostles, as by the tradition of the whole Church, in its sacred declarations
and General Councils."   And again : " The Episcopal rank in the Church as to its primary conferring
was given immediately by Christ to the Apostles
first, as the papal rank to Peter. The Episcopal
rank had in the Apostles and their successors the
use or *exercise* of its own power, subject to Peter,
as Pope, and his successors, *as he had, and they
have, the fontal plenitude of Episcopal authority.*
Wherefore, as concerns such things, those of minor
rank, that is, having cure of souls, are subject to
Bishops, by whom the use of their power is at times
restricted, or stopped, and so it is not to be doubted
can be done by the Pope, in respect to superior
dignitaries, for certain and reasonable causes."

And again he says : " Of which power (of jurisdiction) the plenitude resides in the supreme Pontiff, and is in him entire potentially ; but is derived
to others in degrees, according to the legitimate
determination of that fontal and prime power."[1]

---

[1] Gerson, *De Statibus Ecclesiasticis*, consid. 1, and *De Statu
Prælatorum*, consid. 2 and 3, and *De Protest. Ligandi et Solvendi.*
The last quoted by Ballerini.

The Chancellor Gerson is here only expressing
what had been the unbroken belief down to his
own times, until the great Western schism originated a long train of disasters which have not yet
ceased to agitate Christendom.

But before I pass from this subject, let me say a
word on what is meant by spiritual jurisdiction. It
is a term of law as well as of theology, and it is
desirable to clear up any ambiguity which may
attend its use, if unexplained.

Every Churchman, then, believes that a Priest,
at his ordination, receives certain spiritual powers ;
and, again, a Bishop, at his consecration, certain
others : these are called powers of *order ;* they are
the same in all Priests and in all Bishops re-
spectively. As regards these, S. Peter had no
superiority over his brethren in the Apostolate,
and the Pope has none over his brethren in the
Episcopate. As regards these, one Bishop does
not excel another Bishop, nor one Priest another
Priest. In the whole of the present subject-matter
these powers of *order* do not come into question.

But when a Priest has been ordained, where and
how, in what place, and under what conditions and
restrictions, is he to *exercise* the powers so given
him? All these points the Bishop determines by
assigning to him a particular flock under himself ;
that is, he gives him *mission ;* but he does not
therefore cease to be the *immediate* pastor himself of that flock, over whom he sets another as
subordinate pastor.

And when a Bishop has been consecrated, who

determines where and how, in what place, and under what conditions he is to *exercise* the powers which he has received ? That is, who gives the Bishop *mission ?* who appoints such and such a person to fill such and such a particular diocese?

This power to give *mission* is purely spiritual, eminently and in the highest degree a gift of our Lord ; and upon it depend *for their exercise* all powers whatever which our Lord has committed to His Church for the salvation of souls, and the building of His mystical body.

Will any honest mind, will any one who loves his Saviour, any one who has the spirit of a freeman in his soul, endure that this power of *mission* should be seized upon and appropriated by the civil Government of a State?

But what is the Catholic answer to the question, " Who gives the Bishop mission ? " I will give it in the words of an author to whom I am under great obligations.

"' Episcopal jurisdiction cannot be given, save by the Pope alone or by the whole Episcopal body united with the Pope. Let us go to the origin of things. The power to govern populations in order to their eternal salvation, to instruct them, to oblige them to obedience, to bind them by spiritual penalties, in a word, ecclesiastical jurisdiction, was certainly given by Jesus Christ, nor in its origin could it be given by any other than by Him. We are speaking of men united in one society for the spiritual end of eternal salvation, which society is called the Church ; we are speaking of flocks purchased by the supreme and eternal Shepherd at the priceless cost of His own blood. We are speaking of a kingdom which is a spiritual kingdom of His own acquiring, recovered from the power of darkness by the victory of the cross and the glorious triumph over hell. Lastly, we are speaking of populations which the Divine Father has bestowed on His Son made man, giving to Him all power over them. Now, to whom did Jesus Christ condescend to impart this power? To S. Peter alone before any other ; next to all the Apostles, comprising therein S. Peter marked out to be, and made, their head. We read not in the word of God, written or handed down, and it is certain that Jesus Christ gave not of Himself immediately to any other this power. The sacred text notes expressly, that when Jesus Christ conferred the power of governing His Church, there were only present the eleven Apostles, and He directed His words only to them. The Evangelist S. Matthew notices the remarkable circumstance that Jesus Christ commanded the eleven Apostles to go into Galilee to a place apart, where He appeared, and gave them their mission to instruct and baptise all nations. Accordingly, the power to govern the Church, which in due propagation of the Episcopate was communicated from hand to hand to others, and has been perpetuated unto us, was by Jesus Christ, before He ascended into Heaven, given to the eleven Apostles only, and could not be conferred on others, save by one of the Apostles, who alone had it immediately from

Jesus Christ. Bishops, *considered as individuals*, do not succeed to the Apostles in the *fulness* and *universality* of the Episcopate. There is only the Roman Pontiff, successor of S. Peter, and the whole Episcopal body with the Roman Pontiff at its head succeeding to the Apostolic College, which possess the Episcopate in all its *fulness*, *universality*, and *sovereignty*, as it was instituted by Jesus Christ. Accordingly, there is only the Roman Pontiff, and the whole Episcopal body, which has for subjects all Christians, and which extends its jurisdiction over the whole Church. Hence by necessary consequence it follows that the Roman Pontiff alone, or the whole Episcopal body, can assign subjects to be governed, and confer Episcopal jurisdiction. Every one else who attempts to do this over subjects not his own, does an act essentially, and of its own intrinsic nature, null and void, since *no one gives what he has not got.*" [1]

I will add another passage which seems calculated specially to meet Anglican misconceptions of Church government : " Jesus Christ did not divide His flock into so many portions, nor the world into so many dioceses, assigning one to John, one to Andrew, one to Matthew, etc. *He conferred the Episcopate on S. Peter in all its fulness and sovereignty, and thus He conferred it too on all the Apostolic College, that is, presided over by S. Peter; each Apostle had a full and universal*

---

[1] Bolgeni, *L'Episcopato*, c. vii. s. 81.

power in the whole Church, but with subordination to S. Peter. The Apostles were the first to make a division of nations and dioceses, according as the seed of God's Word bore fruit, and the Christian religion acquired followers through all the earth. Of the Bishops created by the Apostles, some were not fixed to any people or determinate place, but were sent hither and thither according as the need of Christians required. These Bishops acted by an authority delegated from the Apostles, therefore they received it immediately from the Apostles, who had received it from Jesus Christ. Others again were settled in a determinate see, and had assigned a determinate territory to govern; these had a fixed and ordinary jurisdiction, but it is plain that they received it immediately from the Apostles, who constituted them Bishops rather in one place than in another, rather over one people than over another. The disciples of the Apostles pursued the same method in the further propagation of the Episcopate; and by the multiplication of Bishops dioceses became more and more restricted, and the jurisdiction of each Bishop was reduced to more confined limits. It is, then, plain that this jurisdiction was conferred immediately by those who instituted the Bishops, and assigned them to this or that determinate people; and as these institutors acted according to the instructions and the discipline received from the Apostles, so in origin the jurisdiction descended from the Apostles, and from S. Peter, who had received it immediately from Jesus Christ. Thus the streams,

however multiplied in their course, as S. Cyprian
says, parting themselves to irrigate this or that
plot, and springing one from the other, if you
mount upwards, still are found all parted from one
fountain, which gave to them the first waters and
the first impulse to their movement." [1]

Let us only add to this, that he who received
the charge, " Feed My sheep," did not cease to be
their proper pastor, because he divided them among
himself and his brethren, any more than the Bishop,
when he commits a portion of his flock to a Priest
under him, ceases to be his proper pastor ; and as
that commission was to last for ever, forasmuch
as it included all others in itself, and to have a
perpetual succession, because the Church founded
on him who held it was never to fail, so his successor ceased not to have a full and proper power
" to feed, to rule, and to govern the Universal
Church." [2]

He therefore it is, as the head of the whole
Church, and representing it, who gave mission in
ancient times to the Sees of Rome, Alexandria,
and Antioch, and to all others descending from
them ; and he in modern times who gives mission
to all Bishops directly from his own person ; in
both cases' the fountain-head dwelt in himself un-
diminished ; and this is that universal,. immediate,
and supreme jurisdiction which is the proper
nature of the Primacy.

[1] Bolgeni, *L'Episcopato*, s. 94.
[2] *Definition of the Council of Florence.*

SECTION V.

THE CHURCH'S WITNESS TO THE PRIMACY.

WE have now then considered the Primacy of S. Peter's See as a power in present possession, acknowledged by many various nations, continued on by a most wonderful providence of God, wholly without a parallel, for eighteen hundred years, unchanged while everything else around has changed again and again, that is, empires, races, manners, civilisation, literature, the centre of political power, the centre of moral gravity; a power still existing, which has seen all the monarchies of Europe arise as children around it, and all the nations of Europe come to its feet for instruction; and which therefore presents itself with every claim to consideration which a power can have; with a right, moreover, to interpret in its own favour, if indeed that be needful, expressions in ancient authors concerning it, which refer to its headship, without defining it.

We have seen, moreover, that this power is based, not on any grant of the Church of God, not on any concessions of its Bishops from age to age, but on the express words of the Founder of that Church, words so remarkable that they prove

6

themselves to be His who spake as never man spake, in that while they convey the supreme power which is to rule and guide that Church for ever, to be seated at its heart, and to move its hands, they enfold in themselves the living germ from which all its organisation has sprung. In them a root is planted by the Maker of all things, which contains potentially the tree with all its wide-spreading branches, down to the minutest leaf of its vast and varied foliage.

Thirdly, the end and object for which this central power is created has been set forth; that unity of faith and of communion, that building up of the Mystical Body to the measure of the stature of the perfect man, which is a primary purpose of our Lord's Incarnation, and points to a glory only to be revealed at the "restitution of all things."

Fourthly, the nature of this power has been explained as consisting in a universal, immediate, and supreme jurisdiction over the whole Church; such as the very words of institution themselves convey, and such as is imperatively demanded to fulfil the purpose for which the Lord created the power; nay, for which He Himself became incarnate.

One thing only remains, to show that the Church has borne witness, throughout her existence, to a power which she did not create, the secret of her own union, vigour, and strength. This has only been done in a few instances at present, though these are among the most decisive which antiquity supplies. But I proceed to give abundant proof to every candid mind of what I have heretofore laid down.

The Primitive Church, during nearly three centuries, in which it was exposed to continual persecution, was never assembled in a General Council. During that time it was governed by its own Episcopate, cast into the shape which it had received from the moulding hand of S. Peter himself, at the head of the Apostolic College. That Apostle, in his own lifetime, established three primatial Sees, of Rome, Alexandria, and Antioch, —the mother Churches of three great patriarchates, which, as Church after Church was propagated from them, and received its Bishop, yet retained over them a parent's right of correction and inspection. Of these, the two latter, the Sees of Alexandria and Antioch, were subordinate to the See of Rome, to whose Bishop their Bishops were accountable for the purity of their faith, and the due government of their Church. The records of these three first centuries have in a large degree perished ; but we see standing out of them certain facts, which cannot be accounted for but by the Roman Primacy, *viz.*, that the Bishop of Rome, and he alone, claims a control over the Churches of the whole world, threatening to sever from his communion (and sometimes carrying that threat into execution) such as do not maintain the purity of that faith which he is charged to watch over, and the rules of that communion which had come down from the

Apostles.   The well-known instances of S. Clement
writing to the Church of Corinth to heal its divisions, in the very lifetime of S. John, of S. Victor
censuring the Asiatic, and S. Stephen the African
Churches, and of S. Dionysius receiving an apology
for his faith from his namesake, the Bishop of
Alexandria, are sufficient proofs of this.   The
force of the fact lies in this, that the Bishop of
Rome, and he alone, claims, as need may arise,
a control over all; but no one claims a control
over him.

But as soon as the ages of persecution are past,
as soon as the Church Catholic is allowed to develop
free action as one corporate whole, and to exert the
powers which God had planted within her, S. Peter
is found on the throne of the Roman Pontiffs,
superintending, maintaining, consolidating her outward framework and her inward faith.

In the year 325, at the great Nicene Council, the
pre-eminent authority of the Bishops of Rome,
Alexandria, and Antioch, is acknowledged, the
former of these being referred to as a type to
sanction a claim of the latter over his subject
Bishops, and it is stated that "the Roman Church
always had the primacy."   The Bishop of Corduba,
in Spain, apparently at once Papal Legate and
Imperial Commissioner, and Vitus and Vincentius,
Legates of S. Sylvester, presided over the Council;
and "it was determined that all these things should
be sent to Sylvester, Bishop of the city of Rome,"[1]

----

[1] *Codex Canonum Sedis Apostolicæ*, S. Leo, tom. iii. p. 46, edit.
Ballerini.

for his confirmation, which only could make the Council ecumenical, as may be seen even from the fact that of three hundred and eighteen Bishops twenty-two alone belonged to Europe.

In the year 347, a great Council was held at Sardica, intended to be ecumenical. It was presided over by the same Bishop of Corduba, and in its synodical letter to Pope Julius, tells him, "for this will seem the best, and by far the most fitting, if the Lord's Bishops make reference from all the provinces *to the head, that is, the See of the Apostle Peter*." [1]

Thus these two great and most ancient Councils do not in the least *define* the nature of that Primacy which they refer to as an existing fact from the beginning in the Church. So true is that which was stated by a Roman Council of seventy Bishops, under Pope Gelasius, in the year 494, which, after naming the canon of Scripture, the present Roman canon, says, " next to all these Scriptures of the Prophets, Evangelists, and Apostles, on which the Catholic Church by the grace of God is founded, this too we think should be remarked, that though all the Catholic Churches throughout the world be but one bridal-chamber of Christ, yet the holy Roman Catholic and Apostolic Church has been preferred to the rest by no decrees of a Council, but has obtained the Primacy by the voice in the Gospel of our Lord and Saviour Himself, saying : ' Thou art Peter,' etc.

---

[1] Mansi, iii. 40.

" To whom was given also the society of the most blessed Apostle Paul, the vessel of election, who on one and the same day suffering a glorious death with Peter in the city of Rome, under Cæsar Nero, was crowned ; and they alike consecrated to Christ the Lord the above-named holy Roman Church, and as such set it above all the cities in the whole world by their presence and venerable triumph.

" First, therefore, is the Roman Church, the See of Peter the Apostle, ' not having spot, or wrinkle, or any such thing.'

" But second is the See consecrated at Alexandria, in the name of blessed Peter, by Mark, his disciple and Evangelist, who was sent by Peter the Apostle into Egypt, taught the word of truth, and consummated a glorious martyrdom.

" And third is the See held in honour at Antioch in the name of the same most blessed Apostle Peter, because that he dwelt there before he came to Rome, and there first the name of the new people of the Christians arose." [1]

I now, then, proceed to bring witnesses to the seven following points, which I hope to prove in order :

I. A general supremacy in the Roman See over the whole Church ; a supremacy exactly the same in principle with that which is now claimed.

II. The grounding of this supremacy on the attribution of Matt. xvi. 18, Luke xxii. 31, and

---

[1] Mansi, viii. 149.

John xxi. 15, in a special sense to the Pope, as successor of S. Peter.

III. The original derivation of Episcopal Jurisdiction from the person of Peter, and its perpetual fountain in the See of Rome as representing him.

IV. The Papal supremacy over the East, acknowledged by its own rulers and Councils before the separation.

V. The Pope's attitude to Councils, as indicating his rank.

VI. His confirmation of Councils.

VII. The necessity of communion with the Pope.

In so wide a field I can but select the more eminent proofs; but they will be enough to convince all who are capable of conviction.

I. And first, as to general supremacy, I will take the testimony of the great Ecumenical Councils from the third in the year 431, to the eighth in the year 869, for these were all composed of Eastern Bishops, the Papal Legates being often the only, or nearly the only, Westerns present; besides, therefore, their intrinsic authority, they supply a proof that what was stated before them without contradiction, and by them, in favour of the great Western See, was quite indisputable. If any could have disputed it, they would: for "they were all held in the East, by Bishops of the East, under the influence of the Emperors of the East." [1]

The third Council was held at Ephesus in 431,

---

[1] Guizot, *Civilisation en France*, 12 leçon.

to judge Nestorius, Archbishop of Constantinople. It was presided over by S. Cyril of Alexandria, by a special commission from Pope Celestine, and besides was attended by three Papal Legates. The following are some of their proceedings in the Council :

"Arcadius, Bishop and Legate of the Roman Church, said : 'Let your Blessedness order to be read to you the letters of holy Pope Celestine, Bishop of the Apostolic See, and to be named with all veneration, which have been brought by us, by which your Blessedness will be able to learn *what care he bears for all the Churches*.'" [1]

In these letters is said : "We have directed, according to our solicitude, our holy brethren and fellow-Priests, men of one mind with us and well approved, Arcadius and Projectus, Bishops, and Philip our Presbyter, who shall be present at your acts, *and shall carry into effect what we have before determined; assent to whom we doubt not will be accorded by your Holiness*." [2]

This means that the Pope had already condemned Nestorius, and deposed him, unless he retracted ; which throws light on the following sentences of the Council on him :

"*Compelled* by the sacred canons *and the letter of our most holy father and fellow-minister, Celestine*, Bishop of the Roman Church, we have with tears come *of necessity* to this painful sentence against him." [3]

[1] Mansi, iv. 1282.   [2] Coustant., *Ep. Rom. Pont.*, 1162.
[3] Mansi, iv. 1211.

Farther on—" Philip, Presbyter and Legate of the Apostolic See, said : ' We return thanks to the holy and venerable Council, that the letters of our holy Pope having been read to you, you have joined yourselves *as holy members to a holy head.* For your Blessedness is not ignorant *that the blessed Apostle Peter is head of the whole faith, and of the Apostles likewise.*' " [1]

And again, after hearing the acts against Nestorius read, the same says : " It is doubtful to no one, *but rather known to all ages, that holy and most blessed Peter, prince and head of the Apostles, pillar of the faith, and foundation of the Catholic Church, received from our Lord Jesus Christ, Saviour and Redeemer of the human race, the keys of the kingdom of Heaven, and that the power of loosing and binding sins was given to him; who to this very time and for ever lives, and exercises judgment in his successors.* And so our most blessed Pope Celestine the Bishop, his successor in due order, and holding his place, has sent to this holy Council us to represent him." [2]

S. Cyril, having heard this declaration of the Legate, moved that he and the other Legates, " since they had *fulfilled what was ordered them* " by Pope Celestine, should set their hands to the deposition of Nestorius, " and the holy Council said : Inasmuch as Arcadius and Projectus, Legates, and Philip, Presbyter and Legate of the Apostolic See, *have said what is fitting*, it follows that they should also subscribe and confirm the acts."

[1] Mansi, iv. 1290.   [2] *Ibid.*

S. Cyril, most zealous of all men for the rights of the Eastern Church, saw nothing strange in what is here said of the Pope.

In the year 451 the great Council of Chalcedon was called to censure the heresy of Eutyches. S. Leo had, in a letter to Flavian, Archbishop of Constantinople, laid down the true faith; and he speaks in the following letter to the Council of the obedience which he expected to be rendered to his decision.

" In these brethren, Paschasinus and Lucentius, Bishops, Boniface and Basil, Presbyters, who have been sent from the Apostolic See, let your Brotherhood deem me to preside over· the Council, my presence not being disjoined from you, for I am there in my representatives, and long since have not been wanting in setting forth the Catholic Faith : for you cannot be ignorant what from ancient tradition we hold, and so cannot doubt what we desire. Wherefore, most dear brethren, *rejecting altogether the boldness of disputing against the faith inspired from above, let the vain unbelief of those who are in error be quiet, nor venture to defend what may not be believed ; inasmuch as, according to the authorities of the Gospel, the words of the Prophets, and the Apostolic doctrine, it has been most fully and clearly declared, in the letter we have sent to the Bishop Flavian of happy memory, what is the pious and sincere confession concerning the mystery of the Incarnation of our Lord Jesus Christ.*" [1]

Dioscorus, Archbishop of Alexandria, and

[1] S. Leo, *Ep.* 93.

president of the Council at Ephesus two years
before, had taken his place among the Bishops ;
but at the very opening of the Council, Paschasinus,
Legate of the Apostolic See, said : " We have in our
hands the commands of the most blessed and
Apostolic man, Pope of the city of Rome, *which is the
head of all Churches, in which his Apostleship has
thought good to order that Dioscorus should not sit in
the Council,* but be introduced to make his defence."
And Lucentius, another Legate, gives the reason :
" He must give an account of the judgment he
passed ; inasmuch as, not having the right to judge,
he presumed, and *dared to hold a Council without
the authority of the Apostolic See, which never was
lawful, never has been done.*" [1]

And Dioscorus takes his seat as a criminal.

The condemnation of Dioscorus is afterwards
passed in the following terms by the Pope's Legates :
" Paschasinus,—and Lucentius,—and Boniface,—
pronounced. *Leo,* most holy and blessed Archbishop of great and elder Rome, *by us, and by this
holy Council, together with the most blessed Apostle
Peter, who is the Rock and ground of the Catholic
Church, and the foundation of the right faith,* hath
stripped him as well of the rank of Bishop, as also
hath severed him from all sacerdotal ministry." [2]

All assent to this.

Moreover, the Council subscribes to every particle
of S. Leo's letter.

I have already given above the substance of their
letter to him. No stronger terms can be found to

---

[1] Mansi, vi. 579, 582.   [2] *Ibid.,* 1047.

express the supremacy than those there voluntarily tendered to him.

Anatolius, Patriarch of Constantinople, humbly assures him, as the Council had done, "that all the force of the acts and their confirmation had been reserved to the authority of your Blessedness."[1] Notwithstanding, S. Leo confirms their decrees only as to matters of faith, and refuses the canon about the See of Constantinople.

Thus the full Papal Supremacy is set forth in these two Councils, held at the most flourishing period of the ancient Church ; and not only so, but it is recognised as existing from the beginning, and founded on the prerogatives given by our Lord to Peter, whose person is viewed as continued on in his successors ; and the grant of infallibility, deposited in the Church, is not obscurely declared to be seated in the person of her chief.

The two opposed heresies of Nestorius and Eutyches had distracted the East for more than two centuries after the Council of Chalcedon. At length, in the year 680, the sixth General Council meets at Constantinople, to censure the Monothelite error, the last refinement of Grecian subtlety upon the grosser form of Eutyches. The Roman empire of the West had long fallen ; the political estrangement between the two parts of Christendom much increased. But the acknowledgment of the Pope's headship is as definite as ever.

Pope Agatho writes thus to the Emperor :

" Peter, who, by a triple commendation received

[1] S. Leo, *Ep.* 132.

the spiritual sheep of the Church from the Redeemer of all Himself, to be fed by him; under
whose safeguard this his Apostolical Church hath
never turned aside from the path of truth to any
error whatsoever; whose authority, as of the Prince
of all the Apostles, the whole Catholic Church at
all times, and the universal Councils faithfully embracing, have in all respects followed." [1]

His letter is read in the Council, and approved;
and it answers him thus:

"Greatest diseases require stronger remedies, as
you know, O most Blessed; and therefore Christ,
our true God, the Virtue truly Creator and Governor
of all things, hath given us a wise physician, your
Holiness, honoured of God; who firmly repellest
the contagious plague of heresy by the antidotes of
orthodoxy, and impartest the strength of health to
the members of the Church. And therefore we
willingly leave what should be done to you, as
Prelate of the first See of the Universal Church,
standing on the firm rock of faith, having read
through the letter of a true confession sent by your
Paternal Blessedness to our most religious Emperor;
*which we recognise as divinely written from the
supreme head of the Apostles."* [2]

A hundred years later, in 789, Pope Hadrian
writes to Tarasius, the newly-elected Patriarch of
Constantinople, a letter, which is read in the
seventh General Council, and expressly approved
and accepted both by the Archbishop and the
Council. He begins by speaking of "the pastoral

[1] Mansi, xi. 239.　　　[2] *Ibid.*, 683.

care with which it befits us to feed the people of God ;" goes on to say, that only the correctness of faith in Tarasius allowed him to overlook the irregularity of his promotion from a layman ; and then, after quoting " Thou art Peter," adds, " whose See is conspicuous, as holding primacy over the whole world, and is the head of all the Churches of God. Whence the same blessed Apostle Peter, by, the charge of the Lord feeding the Church, hath left nothing out of his range, but always hath held and holds the headship. To which, if your Holiness desires to adhere, and with a pure and un-corrupt mind, in the sincerity of your heart, studies to keep the sacred and orthodox mould of doctrine delivered by our Apostolic See," [1] etc.

This seventh Council, rejecting a former great Council of some hundred Bishops, held thirty years before at Constantinople, from being general, says :

" How was it great and universal? for it had not the countenance of the Roman Pope of that time, nor of the Bishops who are about him, nor by his Legates, nor by an encyclical letter, *as the law of Councils requires.*" [2]

But far more remarkable yet are the proceedings of the eighth Council, in 869, as if Providence had willed that before the Greek schism was accom-plished, the strongest possible testimony against itself, and for that authority which it would be led in self-defence to deny, should be borne by the Patriarchs and Bishops of the East.

---

[1] Mansi, xii. 1077-1084. [2] *Ibid.*, xiii. 207.

At the beginning of the Council, the Papal Legates require that every Bishop should sign and deliver to them for transmission to the Pope a profession of faith, similar in its chief parts to that which had been sent more than three hundred years before from Pope Hormisdas to the Patriarch of Constantinople, after the schism of Acacius, on signing which the Patriarch and all the Bishops of the East were readmitted to communion.

The Legates are obeyed. The profession runs thus:

"Because the sentence of our Lord Jesus Christ cannot be passed by, who says: 'Thou art Peter, and upon this rock I will build My Church,' these words are proved by the real effect which has followed; because in the Apostolic See the Catholic religion has ever been kept immaculate, and holy doctrine celebrated there. Wherefore, by no means desiring to be separated from its faith and doctrine, and following in all things the constitutions of the Fathers, and chiefly of the holy Prelates of the Apostolic See, we anathematise all heresies. . . . Condemning, particularly, Photius and Gregory of Syracuse, *parricides*, that is, *who have not feared to put out their tongue against their Spiritual Father*. Since, following in all things the Apostolic See, and observing in all things its constitutions, we hope that we may be worthy to be in one communion, which the Apostolic See sets forth, *in which is the complete and true solidity of the Christian religion*. But this my profession I (such a Bishop) have written with my own hand, and delivered to thee, most holy Hadrian, Supreme Pontiff and Universal Pope."[1]

The following letter of S. Ignatius, Patriarch of Constantinople, to Pope Nicholas, was also read and approved in the Council. It begins:

"Of the wounds and sores of human members art has produced many physicians; of whom one has treated this disease, and another that, using in their experience amputation or cure. But of these, which are in the members of our Saviour Christ and God, the Head of us all, and of His spouse the Catholic and Apostolic Church, the Supreme Chief and most powerful Word, Orderer, and Healer, and Master, the God of all, hath produced one singular, pre-eminent, and most Catholic Physician, your fraternal Holiness and paternal Goodness. Wherefore He said to Peter, the great and supreme Apostle: 'Thou art Peter,' etc. And again: 'I will give to thee the keys,' etc. For such blessed words He did not, surely, according to a sort of lot, circumscribe and define to the prince of the Apostles alone, but transmitted by him to all who, after him, according to him, were to be made supreme pastors, and most divine and sacred Pontiffs of olden Rome. And therefore, from of old and the ancient times, when heresies and contradictions have arisen, many of those who preceded there your Holiness and supreme Paternity, have many times been made the pluckers-up and destroyers of evil tares, and of sick members, plague-

---

[1] Mansi, xvi. 27.

struck and incurable : being, that is, successors of
the prince of the Apostles, and imitating his zeal in
the faith, according to Christ : and now in our times
your Holiness hath worthily exercised the power
given to you by Christ." [1]

This letter also of Pope Nicholas to the Emperor
Michael, was read and approved in the Council.

" That headship of divine power, which the
Maker of all things has bestowed on His elect
Apostles, He hath, by establishing its solidity on
the unshaken faith of Peter, prince of the Apostles,
made his see pre-eminent, yea, the first. For, by
the word of the Lord it was said to him, ' Thou art
Peter,' etc. Moreover, Peter so entirely ceases not
to maintain for his own people the structure of the
Universal Church unshaken and rooted in the
strength of faith, from the firmness of the Rock,
which is Christ, that he hastens to reform by the
rule of right faith the madness of the wandering.
For, according to the faithful maintenance of the
Apostolical tradition, as yourselves know, the holy
Fathers have often met, by whom it has both been
resolved and observed, that without the consent of
the Roman See and the Roman Pontiff no
emergent deliberation should be terminated." [2]

To Photius himself Pope Nicholas says, as read
in the Council, after setting forth the Primacy in
like terms :

" Because the whole number of believers seeks
doctrine, and asks for the integrity of the faith,

and those who are worthy solicit the deliverance from crimes from this holy Roman Church, which is the head of all Churches, it behoves us, to whom it is intrusted, to be anxious, and the more fervently to be set on watch over the Lord's flock,"[1] etc.

And this letter of the same Pope to the Archbishops, Metropolitans, and Bishops, subject to the See of Constantinople, is also read in the Council.

"Wherefore, because, as your wisdom knows, we are bound by the care of all Christ's sheep, holding through the abundance of heavenly grace his place, to whom is especially said by God, 'Feed My sheep;' and, again, 'And thou, when thou art converted, confirm thy brethren;' we could not so dissimulate or neglect, but that we should visit our sheep dispersed and scattered, and confirm in the faith and good conduct our brethren and neighbours."[2]

Lastly, in its second Canon, the Council itself enacts:

"Obey those set over you, and be subject to them, for they watch for your souls, as those that shall give account: thus Paul, the great Apostle, commands. *Therefore*, holding most blessed Pope Nicholas for the organ of the Holy Spirit, as too most holy Pope Hadrian, his successor, we decree and approve that all things, which by them at different times have been set forth and promulged synodically, as well for the defence of the Church of Constantinople as for the expulsion of Photius, be kept and maintained."[3]

[1] Mansi, xvi. 69.　　[2] *Ibid.*, 101.　　[3] *Ibid.*, 160.

And in the twenty-first Canon it forbids even a
General Council "boldly to give sentence against
the supreme Pontiffs of elder Rome."[1]

And here, indeed, one might stop; for supremacy
as to government, and infallibility as to faith, have
been, in these extracts of the ancient Councils,
again and again set forth as belonging to the See
of Rome. What more can be asked?

S. Ambrose, in the year 390, at the head of his
Council of Bishops, thus thanked Pope Siricius, for
condemning the heretic Jovinian, and transmitting
his condemnation to all Churches : "We recognise
in the letter of your Holiness the watchfulness of
the good shepherd, who carefully guards the door
committed to you, and with pious solicitude defends
Christ's fold, worthy whom the Lord's sheep may
hear and follow.—And so Jovinian, Auxentius, etc.,
whom your Holiness has condemned, know to be
condemned by us likewise, according to your judgment."[2]

The Decretal Letters of the Popes of the first
three centuries have perished ; but with Siricius, in
the year 384, a complete series of them commences.
They are the public acts of the Church's Chief
Bishop, in his ordinary government, written to
Bishops all over the world, and accepted as laws
by them to whom they were written. A learned
writer, who has compiled the most ancient, says of
them : "Out of so many Pontiffs singular for their
learning and holiness, whom I will not say to

---

[1] Mansi, xvi. 174.   [2] *Ibid.*, ili. 664.

charge, but even to suspect, of arrogance or pride,
were rash in the highest degree, not one will be
found who does not believe that this prerogative
has been conferred on himself or his Church, to be
the head of the whole Church. On the other hand,
among so many great Churches of the Christian
world, founded by the Apostles or their successors,
not one will be found whose Prelate was so am-
bitious as to venture to call himself head of the
whole Church." [1]

Let us see how this appears in all the demeanour
and language of these ancient Popes: how exactly
the power which is claimed and exercised now was
claimed and exercised at the end of the fourth
century, and from that time forward, not as a new
thing, but as existing from the first, by our Lord's
institution, and as in full and undisputed operation.

Siricius, A.D. 385, to the Bishop of Tarragona, in
Spain, says : "We bear the burdens of all who
labour, or rather, the blessed Apostle Peter bears
these in us, who in all things, as we trust, protects
and defends us, the heirs of his administration."
And, "you have made reference to the Roman
Church, that is, *the head of your body*." [2]

His successor, Anastasius, to John, Bishop of
Jerusalem, A.D. 400, condemning the opinions of
Origen :

"Certainly I shall not be wanting in care to
guard the faith of the Gospel *in respect to my
populations*, and so far as I am able to hold inter-

---

[1] Coustant., *Prcf.*, p. iii.   [2] *Ibid.*, pp. 624, 637.

course, by letters, *with the parts of my body* over the different countries of the earth."[1]

His successor, Innocent, two letters from whom, so highly praised by S. Augustine, I have given above, speaks, A.D. 410, to the Bishop of Nocera, "as referring to us, *that is, the head and apex of the Episcopate.*"[2]

Pope Celestine, in 430, writes to the clergy and people of Constantinople, harassed by the heresy of Nestorius :

"When I am about to speak to those who make up the Church, let the Apostle's words furnish me with a beginning : 'beside all those things which are without my daily pressure of toil, the care of all the Churches.' So we too, though at a great distance, when *we learnt that our members were being rent* by perverse doctrine, *in our paternal solicitude burning us for you*, were kindled at the fire which was scorching others : although among the Churches of God, which everywhere make up one bridal-chamber of Christ, nothing be distant, nothing can be accounted as foreign. *Since, therefore, you are our bowels,*" etc.[3]

His successor, Xystus, announcing his election to S. Cyril, says : "God hath deigned to call us to the supreme height of the Priesthood."[4]

Pope Zosimus, successor of S. Innocent, and two years after the letters quoted above from him, writes thus in 418, to Aurelius, Primate of Africa, and the Council of Carthage :

---

[1] Coustant., p. 728.   [2] *Ibid.*, p. 910.   [3] *Ibid.*, p. 1131.
[4] *Ibid.*, p. 1231.

"Although the tradition of the Fathers has assigned so great an authority to the Apostolic See, that no one may venture to call in question its judgment, and has maintained this always by its canons and rules, and though ecclesiastical discipline, as shown in the current of its laws, pays the reverence which it owes to the name of Peter, *from whom likewise itself descends :* for canonical antiquity, by the judgment of all, hath willed the power of this Apostle to be so great, from the very promise of Christ our God, that he can loose what is bound, and bind what is loosed ; and an equal power is given to those who enjoy, with his consent, the inheritance of his See ; for he has a care as well for all Churches, as especially for this, where he sat : nor does he permit any blast to shake a privilege or a sentence to which he has given the form and immovable foundation of his own name, and which, without danger to themselves, none may rashly attack : Peter then, being a head of such authority, and the zeal of all our ancestors having further confirmed this, so that the Roman Church is established by all human as well as divine laws and discipline—whose place you are not ignorant that we rule, and hold the power of his name— rather, most dear brethren, you know it, and as Bishops are bound to know it ; such then, I say, being our authority, *that no one can question our sentence,* we have done nothing which we have not of our own accord referred in our letters to your knowledge." [1]

[1] Coustant., p. 974.

But the civil power of that day agreed with the Pope in its estimate of his rights. The following is the edict of the Emperor Valentinian, given when S. Leo met with opposition from Hilary of Arles, in 445.

"Since therefore the merit of S. Peter, who is the chief of the Episcopal coronet, and the dignity of the Roman city, moreover the authority of a sacred Synod, have confirmed the Primacy of the Apostolic See, that presumption may not endeavour to attempt anything unlawful contrary to the authority of that See; for then at length the peace of the Churches will everywhere be preserved, if the whole (*universitas*) acknowledge its ruler. These rules having been kept inviolably hitherto, etc. We decree, by this perpetual command, that no Gallican Bishops, nor those of the other provinces, may attempt to do anything contrary to ancient custom without the authority of the venerable man, the Pope of the Eternal City ; *but let them all deem that a law, whatsoever the authority of the Apostolic See hath sanctioned or may sanction.*" [1]

In the year 499, Pope Symmachus was unjustly accused on a charge of immorality. The Bishops of Italy, whom King Theodoric wished to try him, told the king, "that the person who was attacked ought himself to have called the Council, knowing that to his See *in the first place the rank or chiefship of the Apostle Peter, and then the authority of venerable Councils following out the Lord's command, had*

---

[1] Baronius, *Ann.*, 445.

committed a power without its like in the Churches :
nor would a precedent be easily found to show that
in a similar matter the Prelate of the aforementioned
See had been subject to the judgment of his inferiors." [1]   Even when the Pope sanctioned the
Council, they refused to try him, pronouncing him
" so far as regards men discharged and free, because
the whole matter has been left to the divine judgment."

Yet jealous as they had been of the Pope's
rights, the Bishops of Gaul were in alarm at the
very thought of his being tried.   Their feelings were
expressed in the name of all by the most illustrious
of their number, S. Avitus of Vienne, who, in a
letter to the Roman Senators, Faustus and Symmachus, says : " We were in a state of anxiety and
alarm about the cause of the Roman Church, inasmuch as we felt *that our order was endangered by an
attack upon its head."*   Again, further on, " What
license for accusation against the headship of the
Universal Church ought to be allowed ? "   And,
" As a Roman Senator and a Christian Bishop, I
conjure you that the state of the Church be not less
precious to you than that of the Commonwealth.
If you judge the matter with your profound consideration, not merely is that cause which was
examined at Rome to be contemplated, but as, if
in the case of other Bishops any danger be incurred,
it can be repaired, *so if the Pope of the City be put
in question, not a single Bishop, but the Episcopate*

[1] Mansi, viii. 248.

itself, will appear to be in danger. He who rules the Lord's fold will render an account how he administers the care of the lambs intrusted to him ; but it belongs not to the flock to alarm its own shepherd, but to the Judge. Wherefore restore to us, if it be not yet restored, concord in our chief."[1]

No mediæval Saint, as it seems, understood the Pope's office and universal charge better than S. Avitus.

Ennodius, afterwards Bishop of Ticinum, wrote a defence of this Council, which was so approved as to be put among the Apostolical decrees: in this he says : " God perchance has willed to terminate the causes of other men by means of men ; but the Prelate of that See He hath reserved, without question, to His own judgment. It is His will that the successors of the blessed Apostle Peter should owe their innocence to Heaven alone, and should manifest a pure conscience to the inquisition of the most severe Judge. Do you answer, such will be the condition of all souls in that scrutiny? I retort, *that to one was said :* ' Thou art Peter,' etc. And again, that by the voice of holy Pontiffs, the dignity of his See has been made venerable in the whole world, *since all the faithful everywhere are submitted to it, and it is marked out as the head of the whole Body.*"[2]

The same S. Avitus, writing a few years later to Pope Hormisdas, says : " Whilst you see that it is suitable to the state of religion, and to the full rules

---

[1] Mansi, viii. 293.　　　[2] *Ibid.*, 284.

of the Catholic faith, *that the ever-watchful care of your exhortation should inform the flock committed to you throughout all the members of the Universal Church.* As to the devotion of all Gaul, I will promise that all are watching for your sentence respecting the state of the faith." [1]

And to Senarius, Count of the Patrimony of Theodoric : " You know that it is one of the laws regarding Councils, that in things which pertain to the state of the Church, if any doubt arises, *we should, as obedient members, recur to the supreme Bishop of the Roman Church, as to our head.*" [2]

When Pope Silverius, by a succession of intrigues, had been banished from Rome, under Justinian, in the year 538, he came to Patara, the Bishop of which city went to the Emperor, "and called to witness the judgment of God respecting the expulsion of the Bishop of so great a See, saying that there were in this world many kings, but not one, as that Pope is, over the Church of the whole world." [3]

No one, so far as I know, has ever accused the great Pope Gregory of usurpation, least of all should an Englishman. He wrote to the Emperor of the day :

" To all who know the Gospel, it is manifest *that the charge of the whole Church was intrusted by the voice of the Lord to the holy Apostle Peter,* chief of all the Apostles. For to him is said, ' Peter, lovest thou Me ? feed My sheep.' To him is said, ' Behold,

[1] Mansi, viii. 408.   [2] Gallandi, x. 726.
[3] Baronius, *Annal.*, 538, 13, from *Liberatus Diaconus.*

Satan hath desired to sift you,' etc. To him is said, 'Thou art Peter,' etc. Lo, *he hath received the keys of the kingdom of Heaven, the power of binding and loosing is given to him, the care of the whole Church is committed to him and the Primacy,* and yet he is not called Universal Apostle." [1] S. Gregory well knew that in his own simple title, " Gregory, Bishop, Servant of the Servants of God," everything was conveyed ; he was pre-eminently *the Bishop,* and needed not the titles Ecumenical Patriarch, or Universal Apostle, to set forth his charge of Supreme Shepherd. S. Gregory, like all his predecessors and all his successors, was well assured that the Rock was that single point of the Church which could never be moved. "Who is ignorant," says he, "that the holy Church *is established on the firmness of the chief of the Apostles,* who in his name expressed the firmness of his mind, being called Peter from the Rock ? " [2]

This is again attested by an Eastern, S. Maximus, Abbot of Constantinople, afterwards martyred for the faith. He says in a certain letter concerning Pyrrhus, Patriarch of Constantinople, a chief of the Monothelites, about 650 :

" If he would neither be a heretic, nor be considered one, let him not satisfy this or that person, for this is superfluous and irrational ; since just as when *one* is scandalised by him, *all* are scandalised ; so when *one* is satisfied, *all* beyond a doubt are satisfied too. Let him hasten before all to satisfy

[1] S. Greg., *Ep.*, lib. v. 20.
[2] *Ibid.*, lib. vii. 40.

the Roman See. That done, all will everywhere, with one accord, hold him pious and orthodox. For he merely talks idly when he thinks of persuading and imposing on suchlike as me, and does not satisfy and implore the most blessed Pope of the most holy Roman Church, that is, the Apostolic See, *which from the very Incarnate Word of God, but also from all holy Councils, according to the sacred canons and rules has received and holds in all persons, and for all things, empire, authority, and power to bind and to loose, over the universal holy Churches of God, which are in all the world. For when this binds and looses, so also does the Word in Heaven, who rules the celestial virtues.*"[1]   And just before, "Who anathematises the *Roman See, that is, the Catholic Church.*"

Once more let us take another Eastern, S. Theodore, Abbot of the Studium at Constantinople, who, in the year 809, writes : "To the most holy and supreme Father of Fathers, my Lord Leo, Apostolic Pope :

"Since on the great Peter, Christ our God, after the keys of the kingdom of Heaven, conferred also the dignity of the pastoral Headship, to Peter surely, or his successor, whatever innovation is made in the Catholic Church by those who err from the truth must be referred.—Save us, Arch-pastor of the Church which is under Heaven."[2]

Now, from these testimonies it will be seen that the nature of the supremacy which they set forth is,

[1] Mansi, x. 692.
[2] Baronius, *Annal.*, 809, 14.

a charge of the whole flock of our Lord Jesus Christ, reaching therefore to every need of the flock, not *intruding* on the particular duties of any subordinate pastorship, but embracing, regulating, and maintaining all, so that the same great Pontiff Gregory observes : " As to what he says that he is subject to the Apostolical See, *I know not what Bishop is not subject to it, if any fault be found in Bishops. But when no fault requires it, all are equal according to the estimation of humility :* " [1] who also charges his defensor in Sicily not to meddle with the jurisdiction of Bishops ; and censuring an act of disobedience in another Bishop, tells him : " Had either of the four patriarchs done this, so great an act of contumacy could not have been passed over without the most grievous scandal." [2] And this charge necessarily includes guardianship of the faith, and therefore the supreme judgment in causes touching it, and, by consequence, the gift of not being deceived in that judgment.

It is a dream to imagine any other or lesser Primacy than this, which alone could maintain unity.

II. With regard to the second point, almost every testimony hitherto adduced grounds the Primacy on one or other, or all, of the three sayings of our Lord to Peter, who is invariably regarded as continued on, and living in his successors. And this brings me to the third point.

III. The ordinary government of the Church is

[1] S. Greg., *Ep.*, lib. ix. 59.
[2] *Ibid.*, lib. ii. 52.

perpetually referred back to Peter, as the great type
of the Bishop; in fact, the first Bishop himself, and
of the whole flock, and so the root and origin of the
Episcopate; but as his person was to be continued
on through all his successors, and the Episcopate
to be an ever-subsisting power, so he is viewed as a
living root ever upbearing the tree, and a fountain
ever casting forth its stream.   Let us see this idea,
possessing, as it did in truth, the early Fathers,
carried out from their hints and intimations into
more and more perfect consciousness, till it is
evolved by the complete reason and the fervent love
of a S. Thomas and a S. Bonaventure.

First, Tertullian in the second century : " For if
thou thinkest the Heaven yet shut, remember that
the Lord has left the keys of it to Peter, and *through
him to the Church*." [1]

The whole mind of S. Cyprian seems penetrated
with this thought.   Thus he says :

"This will be " (that is, falling away from the
Church into heresy and schism), "most dear
brethren, so long as there is no regard *to the source
of truth*, no looking *to the head*, nor keeping to the
doctrine of our Heavenly Master.   If any one consider and weigh this, he will not need length of
comment or argument.   It is easy to offer proofs to
a faithful mind, because in that case the truth may
be quickly stated.   The Lord saith unto Peter :
' I say unto thee,' saith He, ' that thou art Peter,'
·etc.   To him again, after His resurrection, He says,

---

[1] *Scorpiace*, 10.

' Feed My sheep.' Upon him, being one, He builds His Church; and though He gives to all the Apostles an equal power, and says, ' As My Father hath sent Me, even so I send you,' etc.; yet in order to manifest unity He has by His own authority so placed the source of the same unity *as to begin from one.* Certainly the other Apostles also were what Peter was, endued with an equal fellowship both of honour and power; *but a commencement is made from unity,* that the Church may be set before us as one; which one Church in the Song of Songs doth the Holy Spirit design and name in the person of our Lord : ' My Dove, My Spotless One, is but one; she is the only one of her mother; elect of her that bare her.' He who holds not this unity of the Church, does he think that he holds the faith? He who strives against and resists the Church, is he assured that he is in the Church? For the blessed Apostle Paul teaches this same thing, and manifests the sacrament of unity, thus speaking : ' There is one Body and one Spirit, even as ye are called in one hope of your calling; one Lord, one Faith, one Baptism, one God.' This unity firmly should we hold and maintain, especially we Bishops presiding in the Church, in order that we may approve the Episcopate itself to be *one* and *undivided.* Let no one deceive the Brotherhood by falsehood; no one corrupt the truth of our faith by a faithless treachery. The Episcopate is one, of which a part is held by each *without division of the whole.* The Church too is one, though she be spread abroad, and multiplies with the increase of her progeny. Even as the sun has rays many, yet one light ; and the tree boughs many, yet its strength is one, seated in the deep-lodged root ; and as, when many streams flow down from one source, though a multiplicity of waters seem to be diffused from its broad overflowing abundance, unity is preserved in the source itself. Part a ray of the sun from its orb, and its unity forbids this division of light ; break a branch from the tree, once broken it can bud no more ; cut the stream from its fountain, the remnant will be dried up.

" Thus the Church, flooded with the light of the Lord, puts forth her rays through the whole world, yet with one light, which is spread upon all places, while its unity of Body is not infringed. She stretches forth her branches over the universal Earth, in the riches of plenty, and pours abroad her bountiful and onward streams ; yet there is one Head, one Source, one Mother, abundant in the results of her fruitfulness."

Now in this famous passage no one can doubt that Cyprian is setting forth the Church Catholic, and his very drift is to prove against heresy and schism that she is *one*, and not only *undivided*, but *indivisible*. What, then, is the counterpart in his mind to the images of the sun's orb, the tree's root, the fountain, the head, and the mother ? What, but the person and See of Peter, with which he began ? It is easy, he says, to offer proofs to faith, because the truth is quickly stated. What truth ? Peter's Primacy, and Universal Pastorship. [1]

---

[1] *De Unitate Ecclesiæ*, 3.

And to this he refers again and again :

" Peter thus speaks, *upon whom the Church was to be built, teaching in the name of the Church.*" [1]

" Peter, whom *first* the Lord chose, upon whom He built His Church." [2]

" Peter, upon whom the Church was founded by God's condescendence." [3]

" One Church founded by Christ the Lord upon Peter in the origin and principle of unity." [4]

" The Lord to Peter *first, upon whom He built the Church, and from whom He instituted and set forth the origin of unity,* gave that power, that what he had 'loosed on Earth should be loosed in Heaven.' " [5]

" God is one, and Christ one, and the Church one, and *one the chair founded upon the rock by the Lord's voice.*" [6]

To Pope Cornelius, of himself, " we know that we exhorted them to acknowledge and to hold by *the root and the womb of the Catholic Church.*"

And to the same :

" They dare to set sail and to carry letters to the Chair of Peter, and that principal Church from which the Unity of the Priesthood took its origin." [7]

" Our Lord speaks in the Gospel, when He is ordering the honour of the Bishop, and the principle of His Church, and says to Peter : ' I say unto thee,' etc. *From this,* through the changes of times and successions, the ordination of Bishops, and the

---

[1] *Ep.* 69.   [2] *Ep.* 71.   [3] *De Bono Patientia.*
[4] *Ep.* 70.   [5] *Ep.* 73.   [6] *Ep.* 40.
[7] *Ep.* 45 and 55.

8

principle of the Church, descends, so that the Church is constituted upon Bishops."[1]

The thought of S. Cyprian is elucidated a little later by S. Optatus. Arguing with a Donatist adversary, he observes:

"You cannot deny that you know that the Chair of Peter *first of all* was fixed in the city of Rome, in which Peter, the *head* of all the Apostles, sat; whence too he was named Cephas; *in which single chair unity was to be observed by all, so that the rest of the Apostles should not each maintain a chair to themselves; and that forthwith he should be a schismatic and a sinner who against that singular chair set up another.*"[2]

And again:

"For the good of unity, blessed Peter both deserved to be preferred to all the Apostles, and *alone received the keys of the kingdom of Heaven, which should afterwards be communicated to the rest.*"[3]

S. Pacian, of Spain, to another Donatist, about the same time:

"He spake to one, *that from one He might shape out unity.*"[4]

S. Ambrose is possessed with the same view. Speaking in the name of the Council of Aquileia, assembled from almost all the provinces of the West, to the Emperor Gratian, he says: "Your Clemency was to be entreated not to suffer the

---

[1] *Ep.* 27.
[2] S. Opt., *cont. Parm.*, lib. ii. c. 6.
[3] *Ibid.*, lib. vii. c. 3.
[4] S. Pacian, *Third Letter to Sempronian*, 26.

Roman Church, the head of the whole Roman world, and that sacred faith of the Apostles, to be thrown into disturbance. *For thence, as from a fountain-head, the rights of venerable communion flow unto all.*"[1]

Meaning, I suppose, that no other particular Church has a right to demand communion with other Churches, unless itself communicate with the Roman Church.[2]

Speaking of the passage, "Thou art Peter," he says: "Because, therefore, Christ, by His own authority, *gave the kingdom,* could He not confirm this man's faith? whom when He calls the rock, He indicates the foundation of the Church."[3] And again: "This is that Peter to whom He said: 'Thou art Peter,' etc. Therefore, *where Peter is, there is the Church*: where the Church is, there is no death, but eternal life."[4]

Peter and the Church are viewed as existing together; and the presence of Peter so living in his successors indicates the Church: and is the foundation, not once, but for ever. As long as the building lasts, the foundation supports it.

At the same time, A.D. 386, Pope Siricius wrote to the Bishops of Africa: "Of Peter, through whom both the Apostolate and Episcopate in Christ took its beginning."[5]

---

[1] Mansi, tom. iv. 622.
[2] See Ballerini, *De Vi ac Ratione Primatus,* c. 31.
[3] *De Fide,* lib. iv. 5.
[4] In *Psal.* xl.
[5] Coustant., p. 651.

In like manner S. Jerome :

" But you say the Church is founded upon Peter ; although in another place this self-same thing takes place upon all the Apostles, and all receive the keys of the kingdom of Heaven, and the strength of the Church is consolidated equally upon them : nevertheless, for this reason *out of the twelve one is selected, that by the appointment of a Head the occasion of schism may be taken away.*" [1]

If a head was necessary for Apostles, how much more for Bishops ! So S. Jerome thought, when he cried from the patriarchate of Antioch to Pope Damasus : " I speak with the successor of the fisherman, and the disciple of the cross. I, who follow none as my chief but Christ, am associated in communion with thy Blessedness, that is, with the See of Peter. On that rock the Church is built, I know. Whoso shall eat the Lamb outside that house is profane. Whoso gathereth not with thee, scattereth : that is, he who is not of Christ is of Antichrist." [2]

And now we are brought to that great Saint who is among the Fathers what Paul is among the Apostles, and S. Thomas among Doctors. Does he recognise S. Peter as the root of Church government, and as continuing on in his successors ?

It would be quite enough to refer to his strong approval of those letters of Pope Innocent, given above, which set forth this idea so plainly. But he speaks in his own person :

[1] Against Jovinian, tom. ii. 279.
[2] To Damasus, *Ep.* 15.

" I am held," he said to a Manichæan, "in the
Catholic Church by the consent of nations and of
races : by authority, begun in miracles, nurtured in
hope, attaining its growth in charity, established in
antiquity. I am held by the succession of Bishops
down to the present Episcopate from the very See
of Peter the Apostle, to whom the Lord, after His
resurrection, intrusted His sheep to be fed. Lastly,
I am held by the very name of Catholic." [1]

Now the force of this third reason lay in the
universality and in the *continuance* of S. Peter's
pastorship.

And to another Manichæan :

" Shall we then hesitate to hide ourselves in the
bosom of that Church, which, even by the confession of the human race, *hath obtained possession
of supreme authority from the Apostolic See*, by the
succession of Bishops, while heretics in vain have
been howling round her, and have been condemned
partly by the judgment of the very people, partly
by the weight of councils, partly also by the majesty
of miracles ? " [2]

But to the Donatists, who enjoyed, and that
without the anxiety of a doubt, the Apostolical
succession, with the full sacramental system of the
Church, as well as her faith, save the point of their
schism, he cries out :

" You know what the Catholic Church is, and
what that is *cut off from the vine ;* if there are any
among you cautious, let them come ; let them find

[1] Tom. viii. 153.
[2] *De Utilit. Cred.*, 17.

life *in the root.* Come, brethren, if you wish to be engrafted in the vine : a grief it is when we see you lying thus cut off. *Number the Bishops even from the very seat of Peter : and see every succession in that line of Fathers : that is, the Rock, which the proud gates of Hell prevail not against."* [1]

Beyond a doubt, then, S. Augustine viewed Peter as continuing on in his successors. But what was his special office as Primate ?

" He saith to Peter, *in whose single person He casts the mould of His Church :* ' Peter, lovest thou Me ?'" [2]

" In single Peter *the unity of all pastors was figured out."* [3]

" For Peter himself, to whom He intrusted His sheep as to another self, *He willed to make one with Himself,* that so He might intrust His sheep to him : that He might be the Head, *the other bear the figure of the Body, that is, the Church."* [4]

" Peter it was who answered, ' Thou art the Christ, the Son of the living God.' *One for many he gave the answer, being the oneness in the many."* [5]

" That one Apostle, that is Peter, first and chief in the order of Apostles, in whom the Church was figured." [6]

" Which Church the Apostle Peter in virtue of

---

[1] *Psalm. in Donatistas,* tom. ix. 7.
[2] *Serm.* cxxxvii. 3, tom. v. 664.
[3] *Serm.* cxlvii. c. 2, p. 702.
[4] *Serm.* xlvi. p. 240.
[5] *Serm.* lxxvi. p. 415.
[6] *Ibid.,* p. 416 g.

the Primacy of his Apostolate represented, *being the type of its universality.*"[1]

"It is said to him, 'I will give to thee the keys of the kingdom of Heaven,' as if he alone had received the power of binding and loosing ; the case really being that he singly said that in the name of all, *and received this together with all, as representing unity itself ; therefore one in the name of all, because he is the unity in all.*"[2]

"The Lord Jesus chose out His disciples before His Passion, as ye know, whom He named Apostles. Amongst these *Peter alone almost everywhere was thought worthy to represent the whole Church. On account* of that very representing of the whole Church, which he alone bore, he was thought worthy to hear : 'I will give to thee the keys of the kingdom of Heaven.' For these keys not one man, but the unity of the Church received. *Here, therefore, the superiority of Peter is set forth, because he represented the very universality and unity of the Church,* when it was said to him : I give to thee, what was given to all. Deservedly also, after His resurrection, the Lord delivered His sheep to Peter himself to feed ; for he was not the only one among the disciples who was thought worthy to feed the Lord's sheep, but when Christ speaks to one, unity is commended : and to Peter above all, *because* Peter is the first among the Apostles."[3]

It would be hard to express the Papal idea more exactly than in these words : " Peter, who is the

[1] Tom. iii. pars ii. 822.   [2] Tom. iii. pars ii. 800.
[3] *Serm.* ccxcv.

mould of the Church," "in whom the unity of all
pastors is figured," "who bears the figure of the
Body, that is, the Church," "the oneness in the
many," "the type of universality and of unity,"
and as such "receiving the keys together with all."

But before leaving the African Church let us
look forward to the year 646, when we find it in a
body writing thus to Pope Theodore:

"To the most blessed Lord, raised to the height
of the Apostolic throne, the holy Father of Fathers,
and the Pontiff supreme over all prelates, Pope
Theodore, Columbus, Bishop of the first See of the
Council of Numidia, and Stephen, Bishop of the
first See of the Byzacene Council, and Reparatus,
Bishop of the first See of the Council of Mauritania,
and all the Bishops of the three above-mentioned
Councils of the province of Africa.

"No one can doubt that there is in the Apostolic
See *a great unfailing fountain, pouring forth waters
for all Christians, whence rich streams proceed,
bountifully irrigating the whole Christian world.*
To this, in honour of the most blessed Peter, the
decrees of the Fathers have assigned all peculiar
reverence, in inquiring into the things of God,
which should everywhere be carefully examined,
but specially by the apostolic head of the prelates
himself, whose solicitude of old it is to condemn
the evil and to approve the good. For by ancient
rules it has been established that whatever was
being carried on," etc.;[1] and then they proceed to

---

[1] Mansi, x. 919.

incorporate that very answer given in 416 by Pope
Innocent to the Council of Carthage, which I have
cited above, which we have seen S. Augustine ap-
proving, and which sets forth the powers of the
Apostolic See, as the living fountain of the Church.

Meanwhile let us glance at the view which the
Greek Fathers have of the person and office of
Peter.

Origen speaks "*of the sum of authority* being
delivered to Peter as to feeding the sheep, and the
Church being *founded upon him as upon the
Earth.*" [1]

Gregory of Nyssa : " *Through Peter* He gave to
Bishops the key of celestial honours." [2]

His brother, S. Basil : " He that, through the
superiority of his faith, received upon himself the
building of the Church ; " and,

" Blessed Peter, selected before all the Apostles,
alone receiving more testimonies and blessings
than the rest, that was intrusted with the keys of
the kingdom of Heaven." [3]

Gregory of Nazianzum : " Do you see, of Christ's
disciples, all being lifted up high, and worthy of
the election, one is called *the Rock, and is intrusted
with the foundations of the Church ?* " [4]

S. Chrysostom, out of many passages : " One
intrusted by Christ with the flock,"—" himself put
in charge of all,"—" Christ put into his hands the

---

[1] *In Rom.*, lib. v. tom. iv. 568.
[2] *De Castigat.*, tom. ii. 746.
[3] *Adv. Eunom.* ii., tom. i. 240, and tom. ii. 221.
[4] *Orat.* xxxii., tom. i. 591.

presidency of the Universal Church,"—" He put
into the hands of a mortal man power over all
things in Heaven when He gave him the keys."

Now the great Eastern Councils, in the next
generation to these Fathers, acknowledge the Pope
as sitting in Peter's seat.

I have already quoted [1] a remarkable letter of
Pope Boniface, in the year 422, which fully sets
forth the idea we are tracing; and another of S.
Leo ; but I add the following :

" To our most beloved brethren, all the Bishops
throughout the province of Vienne, Leo, Bishop of
Rome.

" The Lord hath willed that the mystery of this
gift (of announcing the Gospel) should belong to
the office of all the Apostles, on *the condition of its
being chiefly seated in the most blessed Peter*, first of
all the Apostles: *and from him, as it were from the
Head, it is His pleasure that His gifts should flow
into the whole Body*, that *whoever dares to recede
from the Rock of Peter may know that he has no part
in the divine mystery. For him hath He assumed
into the participation of His indivisible unity, and
willed that he should be named what He Himself
is, saying:* ' Thou art Peter, and upon this Rock I
will build My Church,' *that the rearing of the eternal
temple by the wonderful gift of the grace of God
might consist in the solidity of Peter, strengthening
with this firmness His Church*, that neither the
rashness of men might attempt it, nor the gates of
Hell prevail against it." [2]

[1] See above, sect. 4.   [2] S. Leo, *Ep.* 10.

The Empress Galla Placidia, about the same time, 450, writes to the Emperor Theodosius:
"Let your Clemency give order that the truth of the faith of the Catholic religion be kept immaculate : that according to the form and definition of the Apostolic See, which we also equally venerate as of especial dignity, Flavian remaining in the rank of his priesthood wholly unharmed, judgment be issued by the Council of the Apostolic See, in which he first, who was worthy to receive the heavenly keys, ordered the chiefship of the Episcopate to be." [1]

This was to support the single authority of S. Leo against the regularly called Ecumenical Council of Ephesus, in 449.

In the year 490 Pope Felix III. writes to the Emperor Zeno, praising the newly-elected Patriarch Flavita, for "*referring the commencement of his dignity* to the See of the blessed Apostle Peter ;" and speaks of his letter, in which he wished to be " supported by that power, *from which, at the desire of Christ, the full grace of all Pontiffs is derived*." [2]

Pope Gelasius, in 492, speaks of the See of Peter, "*through which the dignity of all Bishops has ever been strengthened and confirmed*, and for which, by the all-prevailing and peculiar judgment of the three hundred and eighteen Fathers, *its most ancient honour was maintained*. Inasmuch as they remembered the sentence of the Lord." He then

[1] S. Leo, *Ep.* 56.　　　　[2] Mansi, vii. 1098.

quotes the three passages, and goes on, "Why, then, is the Lord's discourse so often directed to Peter? Were not then the other holy and blessed Apostles endued with similar virtue? Who would venture to assert this? But, 'that by the appointment of a head the occasion of schism might be removed,' and that the Body of Christ might be shown to be of one compactness, meeting in one head by the most glorious bond of affection, and that the Church, which should be faithfully believed, might be one, and one the house of the one Lord and one Redeemer, in which we should be nourished of one Bread and one Cup. Wherefore, as I have said, our ancestors, those reverend masters of the Churches, being full of the charity of Christ, *sent to that See in which Peter the Apostle had sat the commencement of their Episcopate, asking from thence the strongest confirmation of their own solidity. In order that by this sight it may be evident to all that the Church of Christ is really in all respects one and indissoluble, which, wrought together by the bond of concord, and the wondrous contexture of charity, is shown to be that robe of Christ, single and undivided throughout, which not even the very soldiers who crucified the Lord dared to part.*" [1]

In a fragment of a letter of the Pope Vigilius, in 538, we have :

"To no one well- or ill-informed is it doubtful that the Roman Church is *the foundation and the mould*

---

[1] Mansi, viii. 75.

of the Churches, from which no one of right belief
is ignorant that all Churches have derived their
beginning. Since, though the election of all the
Apostles was equal, yet a pre-eminence over the
rest was granted to blessed Peter, whence he is
also called Cephas, being the *head and beginning*
of all the Apostles : and what hath gone before in
the head must follow in the members. Wherefore
the holy Roman Church, through his merit consecrated by the Lord's voice, and established by
the authority of the holy Fathers, holds the
Primacy over all Churches, to which as well the
highest concerns of Bishops, their causes, and complaints, as the greater questions of the Churches,
are ever to be referred, as to the head. For he
who knows himself to be set over others should not
object to one being placed over himself. For the
Church itself, which is the first, has bestowed its
authority on the rest of the Churches with this condition, that they be called to a part of its solicitude,
not to the fulness of its power. Whence the causes
of all Bishops who appeal to the Apostolic See,
and the proceedings in all greater causes, are
known to be reserved to that holy See ; especially
as in all these its decision must always be awaited :
and if any Bishop attempts to resist this course, let
him know that he will give account to that holy
See, not without endangering his own rank." [1]

It is natural that the governing power should
speak more fully of itself, but other Bishops express
just the same idea. Thus S. Cæsarius, A.D. 502,

[1] Mansi, ix. 33.

Archbishop of Arles, addressing a series of questions to Pope Symmachus, speaks of the Roman See as the original fountain, and *therefore* the continual guardian of the Church's laws. "*As* from the person of the blessed Apostle Peter the Episcopate takes its beginning, *so* it is necessary that your Holiness should plainly show by competent rules to the different Churches what they are to observe." [1]

And John, Archbishop of Ravenna, speaks to S. Gregory of "that most holy See which *transmits its rights to the universal Church*." [2]

And Stephen, Metropolitan of Larissa, in 531, petitions Pope Boniface for help, reminding him that "Peter, the Father and Doctor of your holy Church, and of the whole world, when the Lord said to him the third time, 'Lovest thou Me? feed My sheep,' *first delivered to you his commission, and then through you bestowed it on all the holy Churches throughout the world*." [3]

In this faith our own Bede was nurtured, who says: "For this blessed Peter, *in a special way*, received the keys of the kingdom of Heaven, and *the headship of judicial power*, that all believers throughout the world may understand, *that whosoever in any way separate themselves from the unity of his faith or of his society, such are not able to be absolved from the bonds of their sins, nor to enter the threshold of the heavenly kingdom*." [4]

The great Archbishop Hincmar, the most vigorous

[1] Mansi, viii. 211.   [2] S. Greg., *Ep.*, lib. iii. 57.
[3] Mansi, viii. 741.   [4] *Homily on S. Peter.*

defender of the rights of the Episcopate in the ninth
century, says :

" In that See the Lord presiding as on His own
throne examines the acts of others, and dispenses all
wonderfully as from His own seat."

And again :

" Catholic Bishops, we decree and judge all things
according to the sacred canons and the decrees of the
Pontiffs of the Apostolic See : the Apostolic See,
and the Catholic Church, in our persons, that are
created Bishops in the stead of Apostles, as in ordering coörders, and in decreeing canonically decrees
together, and in judging judges together with us.
And we who execute the sacred canons and the
decrees of the Pontiffs of the Roman See, under the
judgment of the Apostolic Rock itself, in this nothing else but supporters of those who judge with
justice, and executors of righteous judgments, pay
obedience to the Holy Spirit, who hath spoken
through them, and to the Apostolic See, *from which
the stream of religion, and of ecclesiastical orders and
canonical judgment, has flowed forth.*" [1]

And in the same age, A.D. 847, writes " the
Emperor Lothaire to our most holy spiritual Father,
Leo, Supreme Pontiff, and Universal Pope." " The
supernal disposition hath therefore willed the
Apostolic See to hold the Primacy of the Churches,
which See, through the most blessed Apostle Peter,
in the whole world, on whichever side the Christian
religion is diffused, is the head and foundation of

[1] Hincmar, quoted by Thomassin, *Disc. de l'Eglise*, part i. lib.
i. c. 5.

sanctity, that in whatsoever causes, questions, or matters, the necessity of the Church might advise, all should recur *as to the standard of religion, and the fountain-head of equity.*" [1]

Lastly, Pope Gregory IV., in 830, writes to all Bishops : " We enjoin not anything new in our present orders, but confirm those things which seem of old allowed : as no one doubts, that not merely any pontifical question, but every matter of holy religion, ought to be referred to the Apostolic See as the head of the Churches, *and thence to take its rule whence it derived its beginning, that the head of the institution seem not to be left out, the sanction of whose authority all Bishops should hold, who desire not to be torn from the solidity of the Apostolic Rock, on which Christ has built the Universal Church.*" [2]

And here, before the termination of the ancient discipline, and the separation of the East, and before the introduction of the false decretals, I conclude this line of witnesses, adding only the testimony, four hundred years later, of the two great schoolmen, who in this assuredly, as in a multitude of other instances, have only set forth in their full light principles which had worked from the beginning in the Church. It is the same belief, implicit in S. Augustine, explicit in S. Thomas ; faith but uses reason as her handmaid in the latter to explain what she saw with direct vision in both.

" It is plain that the supreme power of government over the faithful belongs to the Episcopal dignity. But likewise,

[1] Mansi, xiv. 884.   [2] *Ibid.*, xiv. 517.

" 1. That though populations are distinguished into different dioceses and cities, yet as there is one Church, so there must be one Christian people. As, therefore, in the spiritual population of one Church, one Bishop is required to be the Head of the whole population, so in the whole Christian people one is required to be the Head of the whole Church.

" 2. Also, for the unity of the Church it is required that all the faithful agree in faith. But concerning points of faith it happens that questions are raised. Now the Church would be divided by a diversity of opinions, unless it were preserved in unity by the sentence of one. So then it is demanded for the preservation of the Church's unity that there be one to preside over the whole Church. Now it is plain that Christ is not wanting in necessary things to the Church which He loved, and for which He shed His blood, since even of the synagogue it is said by the Lord, ' What more ought I to have done for My vineyard, which I have not done?' (Isa. v. 4). We cannot therefore doubt that one, by the ordering of Christ, presides over the whole Church.

" 3. Further, no one can doubt that the regimen of the Church is best ordered, inasmuch as it is disposed by Him through whom 'kings reign, and princes decree justice' (Prov. viii. 15): now it is the best regimen of the multitude to be governed by one, which is plain from the end of government, namely, tranquillity : for that, and the unity of the subjects, is the end of the ruler. Now one is a more

9

congruent cause of unity than many. Thus it is plain that the regimen of the Church is so disposed that one presides over the whole.

"4. Moreover, the Church militant is drawn by likeness from the Church triumphant, whence John in the Apocalypse saw Jerusalem descending from Heaven, and Moses was told to make all things according to the pattern shown to him in the Mount. Now in the Church triumphant One presides, who presides also over the whole universe, that is, God : as it is said (Rev. xxi. 3) : 'They shall be His people, and God Himself shall be with them, their God.' Therefore, also, in the Church militant there is one who presides over all. This is what is said in Hosea i. 11 : 'Then shall the children of Judah and the children of Israel be gathered together, and appoint themselves one head ; ' and the Lord says, in John x. 16 : 'There shall be one fold, and one shepherd.'

"But should any one object that Christ is the One Head and One Shepherd, who is the One Bridegroom of the One Church, *it is not a sufficient answer*. For it is plain that Christ Himself performs the Church's Sacraments : for He it is who baptises, He who remits sins, He is the true Priest who offered Himself on the altar of the cross, and by whose virtue His body is daily consecrated on the Altar : and yet, because He was not at present to be corporally with all the faithful, He hath chosen ministers by whom He dispenses the aforenamed to the faithful. Therefore, by the same reason, because He was about to withdraw from the Church His corporal presence, it was behoving that He should commit to some one the charge of the Universal Church in His place. Hence it is that He said to Peter, before His ascension : 'Feed My sheep :' and before His passion : 'Thou, when thou art converted, confirm thy brethren :' and to him alone He promised : 'I will give to thee the keys of the kingdom of Heaven,' *that the power of the keys might be pointed out as to be derived through him to others, for the preservation of the Church's unity.*

"But it cannot be said that, although He gave this dignity to Peter, yet it is not derived through him to others. For it is plain that Christ so set up His Church that it should last for ever, according to that of Isaiah ix. 7 : 'He shall sit upon the throne of David, and upon his kingdom, to order it, and to establish it with judgment and with justice from henceforth for ever.' Plain, therefore, is it that He set up in their ministry those who then were, in such a way that their power should be derived unto their successors for the good of the Church unto the end of the world ; especially as He says Himself: 'Lo, I am with you alway to the end of the world.'

"But by this is excluded the presumptuous error of certain persons, who endeavour to withdraw themselves from obedience and subjugation to Peter by not recognising his successor, the Roman Pontiff, as Pastor of the Universal Church." [1]

---

[1] S. Thomas, *Summa contra Gentiles,* iv. 76.

S. Bonaventure adds to this all that is needed :

" Our Lord Jesus Christ, Creator and Governor of all things, when He was about to ascend into Heaven intrusted His Holy Church to His Apostles, for its government and diffusion, principally to the blessed Apostle Peter, to whom He said specially three times, concerning the universal flock of the faithful : ' Feed My sheep.'   But that the Universal Church might be governed in a more ordered manner, the holy Apostles arranged it into Patriarchates, Primacies, Archbishoprics, Bishoprics " (he means the *thing*, not the *names*, for these are later), " Parishes, and other canonical distinctions : that, inasmuch as by one or by few the individual faithful could not be fitly provided with all things necessary to salvation, many might be called to a participation of this care, according to their several limitations, for the good of souls ; and, in proportion to the extent of pastoral care, each one of them too received a certain power of authority, the fulness of ecclesiastical power dwelling in the Apostolic See of the Roman Church, in which the Apostle Peter, Prince of the Apostles, specially sat, and left there to his successors the same power.

" But *threefold* is the fulness of this power, *viz.*, in that the Supreme Pontiff himself *alone* has the whole fulness of authority which Christ bestowed on His Church, and that he has it *everywhere* in all Churches as in his own special See of Rome, and that from him all authority *flows* unto all inferiors throughout the Universal Church, as it is competent for each to participate in it, as in Heaven all the glory of the Saints flows from the very fountain of all good, Jesus Christ, though each share it in different degrees according to their capacity."[1]

The sum of all this is, what age after age is bringing out with more and more distinctness, that the visibility and unity of the Church depend on the Supreme Pontiff; those who reject him maintain neither One Body nor One Spirit.

And it surely adds very greatly to the force of the preceding argument, that on the other side no intelligible view as to the origin and maintenance of mission and jurisdiction in the Church can even be presented to the mind. You search in vain for any antagonist system which will hold together, which will bear to be thought upon, and not run up into confusion and anarchy. What is this, after all, but saying, that a Body requires a Head, and a visible Body a visible Head?

IV. I now come to the fourth point, that the Papal Supremacy over the East was acknowledged by its own rulers and Councils before the separation.

This indeed is already fully involved in the first and second points, but I add a few more special proofs.

The first which I shall bring would seem to render all others needless. In the year 519 was terminated a schism of thirty-seven years, brought

---

[1] S. Bonaventure, *Cur Fratres Minores prædicent*, tom. vii. 366.

about by the wickedness of Acacius, formerly Patriarch of Constantinople, who, with the whole civil power of the Greek Emperor to back him, had communicated with heretics, interfered with the succession of the Patriarchs of Alexandria and Antioch, and caused unnumbered evils to the Eastern Church. By the advice of Acacius, the Emperor Zeno had put forth a decree, called the Henoticon, or preserver of peace, which made it an open question to hold or deny the faith of the Council of Chalcedon ; and he forced the Bishops throughout his empire to sign this. The alleged purpose was to keep both parties, the Eutychean heretics and the Catholics, in the Church. Acacius, for his misdeeds, had been solemnly deposed and excommunicated by Pope Felix ; but he was supported by the Emperor in possession of the See of Constantinople, and other Patriarchs succeeded him ; and the whole East became severed from the West, save that great numbers in all parts adhered to the Roman communion in spite of persecution. At length, in the year 519, peace was restored on these terms : That the Patriarch John, of Constantinople, and all the Bishops subject to him, should sign a formulary, dictated by Pope Hormisdas, in which they professed obedience in all things to the See of Rome, acknowledged in it a primacy by gift of our Lord, which involved perpetual purity of faith and necessity of communion with that See, and anathematised by name their own Patriarch Acacius, and all who had followed him. I have given the form in the proceedings of the eighth Council, where it was used again. The Patriarch John sets forth the one chair of the Episcopate, saying : " I declare the See of the Apostle Peter, and that of the Imperial City (Constantinople), to be one See ; promising for the future that those severed from the com munion of the Catholic Church, that is, not agreeing in all things with the Apostolic See, shall not have their names recited at the sacred mysteries." [1]

Submission more complete can hardly be imagined.

In the year 536 the Emperor Justinian signed the same formulary, and presented it to Pope Agapetus, to clear himself from the imputation of favouring the heresy of Anthimus, Patriarch of Constantinople, whom that Pope had just deposed. He says in it : " Wherefore following in all things the Apostolic See, we set forth what has been ordained by it. And we profess that these things shall be kept without fail, and will order that all Bishops shall do according to the tenor of that formulary : the Patriarchs to your Holiness, and the Metropolitans to the Patriarchs, and the rest to their own Metropolitans : that in all things our Holy Catholic Church *may have its proper solidity.*" [2]

How could the Emperor Justinian express more plainly his belief that the Apostolic See was the rock of the Catholic faith, which indeed is said expressly at the beginning of the formulary ?

---

[1] Mansi, viii. 451.   [2] *Ibid.*, 857.

.. About the year 650, Pope S. Martin exercises his power of universal jurisdiction by constituting John, Bishop of Philadelphia, his Vicar in the East, "that you may correct the things which are wanting, and appoint Bishops, Presbyters, and Deacons in every city of those which are subject to the See both of Jerusalem and of Antioch ; we charging you to do this in every way, in virtue of the Apostolic authority which was given us by the Lord in the person of most holy Peter, prince of the Apostles; on account of the necessities of our time, and the pressure of the nations." [1]

All that I have laid down under the third point is required to justify this exercise of authority.

Again, Pope Gelasius asks why Acacius, Patriarch of Constantinople, "had not been diligent to give in accounts to the Apostolic See, from which he knew *that the care of those regions*" (the East in general) "*had been delegated to him.*" [2]

The following are cases of the confirmation of Eastern Patriarchs by the Roman See :

Pope Celestine confirms Maximianus in the See of Constantinople, after the deposition of Nestorius, A.D. 432.   He writes to him : "Take the helm of the ship well known to you, and direct it, as we know that you have learnt from your predecessors." [3]

The same Pope having written to the Bishops of Alexandria, Antioch, and Thessalonica, authorising the translation of Bishops, provided it were for the

---

[1] Mansi, x. 806.   [2] *Ibid.*, viii. 61.
[3] Coustant., 1206.

general good, Proclus was transferred from Cyzicus to the Patriarchal Chair of Constantinople.[1]

Pope Simplicius (A.D. 482) in his letter to Acacius, Patriarch of Constantinople, says that nothing was wanting to a new Patriarch of Alexandria, *"save that he might receive that establishment in his See which he desired by the assent of our Apostolic rule."*[2] And of the Patriarch of Antioch : "Having embraced, in the bosom of the Apostolic See, the Episcopate of our brother and fellow-bishop Calendion, we take into the number of our fellowship, through the grace of Christ our God, in the union of our order (*collegii*), the prelate of so great a city."

Maximus, Patriarch of Antioch, had been irregularly appointed by Dioscorus, at the Robbers' Council of Ephesus, 449 ; but he is confirmed in his See by S. Leo, at the Council of Chalcedon.

"Anatolius, Archbishop of Constantinople, spoke. We decree that nothing done in that called a Council shall hold good, except concerning most holy Maximus, Bishop of the great city of Antioch ; since most holy Leo, Archbishop of Rome, by receiving him into communion, *hath judged that he should govern the Church at Antioch ;* which prescription I too, following, have approved, and all the present holy Council."[3]

The following refer to appeals :

Pope Boniface I. (A.D. 422), writing to the

---

[1] Socrates, *Hist.*, vii. 39, 40.   Thomassin, *Discipline de l'Eglise*, part ii. lib. ii. c. 61.

[2] Mansi, vii. 991, 992.   [3] *Ibid.*, 258.

Bishops of Thessaly, thus sets forth cases of subjection to his See, which had occurred in the preceding century :

"The care of the Universal Church, laid upon
him, attends the blessed Apostle Peter, by the
Lord's decree ; which indeed, by the witness of the
Gospel, he knows to be founded on himself; nor
can his honour ever be free from anxieties, *since it
is certain that the supreme authority* (summam
rerum) *depends on his deliberation.* Which things
carry my mind even to the regions of the East,
which by the force of our solicitude we in a manner behold. . . . As the occasion needs it, we
must prove by instances that the greatest Eastern
Churches, in important matters, which required
greater discussion, have always consulted the
Roman See, and, as often as need arose, asked its
help. Athanasius and Peter, of holy memory,
Bishops of the Church of Alexandria, asked the help
of this See. When the Church of Antioch had been
in trouble a long time, so that there was continual
passing to and fro for this, first under Meletius,
afterwards under Flavian, it is notorious that the
Apostolic See was consulted. By whose authority,
after many things done by our Church, every one
knows that Flavian received the grace of communion, which he had gone without for ever, had
not writings gone from hence respecting it. The
Emperor Theodosius, of merciful memory, con-
sidering the ordination of Nectarius to want ratification, because it was not according to our rule"
(on account of his being a layman), "sent an

embassy of Councillors and Bishops, and solicited a letter of communion to be regularly despatched to him from the Roman See, *to confirm his Episcopate*. A short time since, that is, under my predecessor Innocent, of blessed memory, the Pontiffs of the Eastern Churches, grieving at their severance from the Communion of blessed Peter, asked by their Legates for reconciliation, as your Charity remembers." [1]

This agrees with what the Greek historian Sozomen tells us, that "the Bishop of the Romans having inquired into the accusations against each" (S. Athanasius, Paul Bishop of Constantinople, Marcellus of Ancyra, and Asclepas of Gaza), "when he found them all agreeing with the doctrine of the Nicene Synod, *admitted them to communion as agreeing with him. And inasmuch as the care of all belonged to him on account of the rank of his See, he restored to each his Church.*" [2]

Pope S. Gregory hears an appeal of an Abbot, John of Constantinople, from the Patriarch John, reverses his sentence, and compels him to receive the Abbot back.[3]

About the year 500, the Bishops of the East, suffering under the schism of Acacius, address Pope Symmachus for relief, begging him to take them to his communion. They say that they supplicate him not on account of the loss of one sheep, having just quoted the parable of the Good Shepherd, but for almost three parts of the world.

[1] Coustant., 1039.   [2] *Hist.*, iii., c. viii.
[3] *Ep.*, lib. vi. 24.

" But do thou, as an affectionate father among children, beholding us perishing by the prevarication of our Father Acacius, not delay : who art daily taught by the sacred doctor Peter to feed the sheep of Christ intrusted to thee throughout the whole habitable world, gathered together, not by force, but of their own accord." [1]

A few years later, on a like occasion, Pope Hormisdas (A.D. 514) is addressed by about two hundred Archimandrites, Presbyters, and Deacons of Syria.

" To the most holy and blessed Patriarch of the whole Earth, Hormisdas, holding the See of Peter, Prince of the Apostles, the entreaty and supplication of the humble Archimandrites and other Monks of the province of Second Syria.

" Since Christ our God *has appointed you Chief Pastor, and Teacher, and Physician of souls*, we beseech you, therefore, most blessed Father, to arise, and justly *condole with the Body torn to pieces, for ye are the Head of all*, and avenge the Faith despised, the Canons trodden under foot, the Fathers blasphemed. The flock itself comes forward to recognise its own Shepherd in you its true Pastor and Doctor, to whom the care of the sheep is intrusted for their salvation." [2]

The following are from a Metropolitan of Cyprus, and a Patriarch suffering under the Monothelites (A.D. 643).

" To the most blessed Father of Fathers, Arch-

---

[1] Mansi, viii. 221.   [2] *Ibid.*, viii. 428.

bishop and Universal Patriarch, Theodore, Sergius, the humble Bishop, health in the Lord.

"Christ our God hath established thy Apostolic See, O Sacred Head, as a divinely-fixed immovable foundation, whereon the faith is brightly inscribed. For 'Thou art Peter,' as the Divine Word truly pronounced, and on thy foundation the pillars of the Church are fixed. Into thy hands He put the keys of the Heavens, and pronounced that thou shouldst bind and loose in Earth and Heaven with power."[1]

The petition of Stephen, Bishop of Dora, first member of the Synod of the Patriarch of Jerusalem, read in the Lateran Council of Pope Martin (A.D. 649).

"Who shall give us the wings of a dove, that we may fly and report this to your supreme See, which rules and is set over all, that the wound may be entirely healed? For this the great Peter, the Head of the Apostles, has been wont to do with power from of old, by his Apostolical or Canonical authority; since manifestly not only was he alone beside all thought worthy to be intrusted with the keys of the kingdom of Heaven, to open and to shut these, worthily to the believing, but justly to those unbelieving the Gospel of Grace. Not to say that he first was set in charge to feed the sheep of the whole Catholic Church; for He says: 'Peter, lovest thou Me? Feed My sheep.' And again, in a manner special and peculiar to himself, having

[1] Mansi, x. 913.

a stronger faith than all in our Lord, and unchange-
able, to convert and confirm his spiritual partners
and brethren, when tossed by doubt, having had
power and sacerdotal authority providentially committed to him by the very God for our sakes
Incarnate.   Which knowing, Sophronius, of blessed
memory, Patriarch of the holy city of Christ our
God, placed me on Holy Calvary, and there
bound me with indissoluble bonds, saying : ' Thou
shalt give account to our God, who on this sacred
spot was willingly sacrificed in the flesh for us,
at His glorious and dreadful appearing, when He
shall judge the living and the dead, if thou delay
and neglect His Faith endangered : though I, as
thou knowest, cannot do this personally, for the
inroad of the Saracens, which has burst on us for
our sins.   *Go then with all speed from one end of the
earth to the other, till thou come to the Apostolic See,
where the foundations of the true faith are laid.*
Not once, not twice, but many times accurately
make known to the holy men there what has been
stirred up among us, and cease not earnestly en-
treating and requesting, till out of their Apostolic
wisdom they bring judgment unto victory.' "[1]

V. The relation of the Roman Bishop to Councils
plainly indicates his rank.

Pope Celestine thus instructs the Legates whom
he was sending to the Third General Council :

"When, by God's help, as we believe and hope,
your charity shall have reached the appointed place,

---

[1] Mansi, x. 894.

direct all your counsel to our brother and fellow-Bishop Cyril" (already deputed to be the Pope's Legate in this matter), "and do whatsoever shall be advised by him ; *and we charge you to take care that the authority of the Apostolic See be maintained.*

" If the instructions given to you tend to this, be present at the Council ; if it comes to a discussion, *you are to judge of their sentences, not to enter into a contest.*" [1]

To the Council itself the Pope writes, as we have seen, that he doubts not they will agree to what he has ordered to be executed.   ·

The Council replies to the Pope : " The zeal of your Holiness in the cause of piety, and your solicitude for the true faith, dear and pleasing to God our Saviour, are worthy of all admiration. For it is your wont, who are so great, to be well approved in all things, and to make the establishment of the Churches the object of your zeal." [2]

They tell him, further, that they had reserved the excommunication of the Patriarch John of Antioch to his judgment.

In like manner S. Leo writes to the Council of Chalcedon, not doubting that they would accept the letter in which he had defined the true faith.

Socrates and Sozomen give us the key to this language. The former speaks of the " Ecclesiastical Canon ordering that the Churches should not make Canons contrary to the sentence of the Bishop of Rome ; " and the latter says, Pope Julius wrote to

---

[1] Coustant., 1152.   [2] *Ibid.*, 1166, 1174.

the Eusebian Bishops, "that it was an hierarchical law to declare null and void what was done against the sentence of the Bishop of the Romans."[1]

Thus we have seen Dioscorus condemned for holding a Council without Pope Leo. And in the Seventh Council (A.D. 787), a previous one of many hundred Bishops is declared not to be Universal, because it had not the presence of the Pope's Legates, "as the law of Councils requires."

From Constantinople S. Theodore Studites writes, about 800, to Pope Leo III.:

" If they, arrogating to themselves authority, have not feared to assemble an heretical Council, *who could not assemble even an orthodox one without your recognition of it* (as the custom from ancient times holds good), how much more just and even necessary were it that a lawful Council should be called by your divine Headship!"[2]

A little later, just before the Greek schism, Pope Nicholas I. wrote to the Emperor Michael :

"Observe that not the Nicene, nor any Council whatever, granted any privilege whatever to the Roman Church, as knowing that in the person of Peter *it had fully received the right of all power, and the regimen of all Christ's sheep*," referring to a letter of Pope Boniface, four hundred years earlier, which had said the like.[3]

VI. But this point is closely connected with the next, the confirmation of Councils. And perhaps

[1] Socr., *Hist.*, ii. 17 ; Soz., iii. 10.
[2] Baronius, *Ann.*, 809, No. 15.
[3] Mansi, xv. 205.

nothing shows more conclusively the imperium over all belonging to the See of S. Peter than this right.

S. Jerome tells us that at the latter part of the fourth century the Roman See was perpetually referred to for its judgment on difficult matters by Councils both of the East and West. " I was secretary to Damasus, Bishop of the Roman city, and answered the synodical consultations of the East and West."[1]

S. Innocent, a few years later, says that nothing was *terminated* without the consent of that See.

But the strongest exertion of this power is, giving that ratification to General Councils, without which they do not express the voice of the Church Catholic. And this power will be sufficiently proved, if some Councils, which would otherwise have been general, were not so, simply from wanting this Papal ratification : and others, not of themselves general, became so, simply from having it.

Of the former class is the Council of Ariminum in 359, attended by more than four hundred Bishops, and whose formulary was signed by the Bishops of the East. Yet in the Council held by Pope Damasus at Rome ten years afterwards, it was declared that the number of Bishops assembled there could not carry force, because the agreement of the Roman Bishop was wanting. And this has been always held since.[2]

Yet more remarkable is the case of the second

---

[1] *Ep.* 123.   [2] *Synodal Letter*, Mansi, iii. 458.

Council of Ephesus, regularly called, attended by all the East, and by the Legates of S. Leo, but annulled by his subsequent opposition to it, and branded as the Robbers' Council.

Of the latter class, a Council held at Constantinople of one hundred and fifty Bishops of the East alone, which set forth the divinity of the Holy Spirit, became the second General Council solely by Pope Damasus accepting its decrees of faith.

A Council held by the influence of Justinian, against the wishes of Pope Vigilius, and bitterly opposed by all the West, became the fifth General Council, because it was subsequently confirmed by Vigilius.

And the influence of the Popes, it is well known, alone induced the West to receive the seventh General Council, where indeed the Papal Legates were the only Westerns who sat.

Again, observe that S. Leo *annuls* the second Council of Ephesus, but *excepts* the ordination of Maximus to Antioch ; and *ratifies* the Council of Chalcedon, but *excepts* the exaltation of the See of Constantinople.

And the third General Council having left to Pope Celestine the decision as to the excommunication of the Patriarch John of Antioch, Xystus, his successor, writes to S. Cyril :

" As to the Bishop of Antioch, and the rest, who with him wished to be partisans of Nestorius, and as to all who govern Churches contrary to the ecclesiastical discipline, *we have already determined this rule*, that if they become wiser, and with their leader reject everything which the holy Council has rejected *with our confirmation*, they are to return into their place as Bishops." [1]

A Council at Rome, held in the year 485, writing to the Clergy of Constantinople, observes with regard to the name of Pope Felix alone being appended to the decree deposing Acacius : " As often as the Priests of the Lord are assembled within Italy for ecclesiastical matters, especially of faith, the custom is retained that the successor of the Prelates of the Apostolic See, in the person of all the Bishops of the whole of Italy, according to the care over all Churches which belongs to him, should regulate all things, for he is the head of all : as the Lord says to blessed Peter : 'Thou art Peter,' etc. *Following which voice, the three hundred and eighteen Fathers assembled at Nicæa left the confirmation and ratification of matters to the holy Roman Church, both of which down to our time all successions by the help of Christ's grace maintain."* [2]

If an assertion thus publicly made, by such an authority, in the absence of anything to contradict it, is not to be believed, very few facts of history are more worthy of credit.

Pope Gelasius, writing to the Bishops of Dardania, in 495, observes : " We trust that no true Christian is ignorant that the appointment of every Council which the assent of the Universal Church has approved ought to be executed by no other See but the first, *which both confirms every Council by its*

---

[1] Coustant., 1238.   [2] Mansi, vii. 1140.

authority, and maintains them by its continued
government, in virtue, that is, of its headship, which
blessed Peter received indeed from the Lord's voice,
but the Church, no less following that voice, hath
ever held, and holds." [1]

Ferrandus, a well-known deacon of Carthage,
writing in 533 to two deacons of the Church of
Rome, says :   .

" It is only the divine precepts in the canonical
books, and the decrees of the Fathers in General
Councils, which are not to be refuted, nor rejected,
but maintained and embraced, according to that
command of Holy Scripture: ' Hear, my son, the
law of thy father, and despise not the advice of
thy mother.' For the law of the father is conspicuous, as it seems to me, in the canonical books :
the advice of the mother is contained in Universal
Councils. The Bishops, moreover, who meet there,
subscribe their own statutes, that no doubt may be
left by whom the discussion has been held : but,
besides these, no further subscription is required :
for it is held to be sufficient for full confirmation,
if, brought to the knowledge of the whole Church,
they cause no offence nor scandal to the brethren,
and are approved to agree with the Apostolic
faith, *being confirmed by the consent of the Apostolic
See."* [2]

VII. And now every witness whom I have
hitherto brought confirms likewise the remaining
point,—the necessity of communion with the Pope.

---

[1] Mansi, viii. 51.   [2] Gallandi, tom. xi. 363.

If his Primacy extends over the whole Church, as its controlling, regulating, maintaining, and uniting power, which supports its discipline, and gives voice to its faith ; if this be by direct gift of our Lord, who conferred upon Peter alone that whole Episcopate, of which others were to hold a part in communion with him and in dependence on him, and as long as this Episcopate endures, the original condition of its existence endures likewise ; if, as having *that* whole and complete in himself of which others have a part, he is the living source and spring of mission and jurisdiction ; if the Eastern Church acknowledged such a Primacy, when the imperial power was proudest in her, and when the See of Rome was politically no longer subject to that imperial power ; if " the Churches may not make canons contrary to the sentence of the Bishop of Rome ; " if his See " confirms every Council by its authority, and maintains them by its continued government ; "—how can he not be the centre of unity, so " that whoever dares recede from the rock of Peter may know that he has no part in the divine mystery " ?[1] Is it any wonder that every Saint is penetrated with this idea? that S. Ambrose cries, " Where Peter is, there is the Church : " S. Jerome, " Whoso gathereth not with thee scattereth : " S. Optatus, " He is a schismatic and a sinner who against that singular chair sets up another : " S. Augustine, " Come, brethren, live in the *root*, be grafted into the *vine*—this is the

---

[1] Socrates, Pope Gelasius, and S. Leo, all in the fifth century.

Rock, which the proud gates of Hell prevail not against:" the whole Oriental Church together, " Those severed from the communion of the Catholic Church, that is, not agreeing in all things with the Apostolic See, shall not have their names recited at the sacred mysteries:" or, again, "We follow and obey the Apostolic See; those who communicate with it, we communicate with—those condemned by it, we condemn:"[1] or, that the Catholic Church of old, assembled in her most numerous General Council, confessed the Bishop of Rome to be the organ of the Holy Spirit dwelling in her, " Leo, most holy and blessed Archbishop of great and elder Rome, *by us and by this holy Council* together with the most blessed Apostle Peter, who is the Rock and Ground of the Catholic Church, and the Foundation of the right faith." Heresy itself, by the voice of one sprung from our own island, in S. Augustine's time spontaneously expressed this. The Briton Pelagius laid his confession of faith before Pope Innocent I. in these words :

" This is the faith, most blessed Pope, which we have learnt in the Catholic Church, and which we always have held and hold. In which if anything perchance is laid down with somewhat of ignorance, or want of caution, we desire to be corrected by you, who hold both the faith and seat of Peter. But *if this our confession is approved by the judgment of your Apostleship*, then whosoever tries to cast a

---

[1] Mennas, Patriarch of Constantinople, at his Council held in 536.

blot on me will prove himself ignorant, or spiteful, *or even not a Catholic,* but will not prove me a heretic." [1]

An early Father, Bishop and martyr in Gaul, but a Greek by birth, and only two steps removed from S. John, has given us the reason of all this : " With this Church (the Roman), *on account of its superiority of headship it is necessary* that every Church should agree, that is, the faithful on every side, in which the tradition from the Apostles has ever been preserved by those who are on every side." [2]

May we not, then, sum up the whole belief of the Church concerning that living power which her Lord has put at her centre in the words of one who has been called the last of the Fathers, who, at least in his day, was loved and honoured by all who themselves were worthy of love and honour ? Thus speaks S. Bernard to that monk who had been his own spiritual child, but was become his father, as holding the See of Peter : and in him speaks a countless multitude of Holy Doctors, Saints, and Martyrs, who have had no other home, hope, or comfort, but in the Church of God, who but carried on what they had inherited, a perpetual living tradition. Thus he interprets S. Augustine : " This is the Rock against which the proud gates of Hell prevail not."

" Come, let us inquire yet more diligently who you are, that is, what person you, for a time, sus-

[1] S. August., tom. x. App. 97.
[2] S. Irenæus, lib. iii. 3.

tain in the Church of God.   Who are you ? a great
Priest, the Supreme Pontiff.   You are chief of the
Bishops, heir of the Apostles, in primacy Abel, in
government Noah, in patriarchate Abraham, in
order Melchizedec, in dignity Aaron, in authority
Moses, in judgment Samuel, in power Peter, in
unction Christ.   You are he to whom the keys are
delivered, to whom the sheep are intrusted.   Others,
indeed, there are who keep the door of Heaven, and
are shepherds of flocks, but you have inherited both
names above the rest, as in a more glorious, so in a
different way.   They have each their several flocks
assigned to them, while to you singly all are intrusted as one flock.   And not only of the sheep,
but of all the shepherds you are the only Shepherd.
Ask you whence I prove this ?   By the word of the
Lord.   For to whom I say, not of Bishops, but
even of Apostles, were all the sheep intrusted so
absolutely, and without distinction ?   ' Peter, if
thou lovest Me, feed My sheep.'   Which sheep?
the people of this or that city, or region, or specified
empire ?   My sheep, He saith.   To whom is it not
plain that He did not designate some, but assign
all ?   nothing is excepted where nothing is distinguished.   And perhaps the rest of his fellow-dis-
ciples were present when, by committing them to
one, He commended unity to all in one flock, and
one shepherd, according to that ' My dove, My
beautiful, My perfect is but one.'   Where is unity,
there is perfection.   The other numbers have not
perfection, but division, in receding from unity.
Hence it is that others received each their own

people, knowing the sacrament. Finally, James, who seemed to be a pillar of the Church, was contented with Jerusalem alone, yielding up to Peter the whole. But well was he there placed to raise up seed to his dead Brother, when that Brother was slain. For he was called the brother of the Lord. Moreover, when the brother of the Lord gives way, what other would intrude himself on the prerogative of Peter ?

" Therefore, according to your canons, others have been called to a part of your solicitude, but you to the fulness of power. The power of others is conferred within certain limits ; yours is extended even over those who have received power over others. Can you not, if fitting cause exist, shut Heaven to a Bishop, depose him from the Episcopate, even deliver him to Satan ? Therefore does your privilege stand to you unshaken, as well in the keys which are given you, as in the sheep which are intrusted to you. Hear another thing which no less confirms to you your prerogative. The disciples were in the ship, and the Lord appeared on the shore, and, what was cause of greater delight, in His risen Body. Peter, knowing that it is the Lord, casts himself into the sea, and thus came to Him while the rest arrived in the ship. What meaneth that ? It is a sign of the one only Priesthood of Peter, by which he received not one ship only, as the rest each their own, but the world itself for his government. For the sea is the world, the ships Churches. Thence it is that, on another occasion, walking like the Lord on the waters, he marked himself out as the single Vicar of Christ, who should rule over not one people, but all ; since the ‘many waters’ are ‘many peoples.’ Thus, while every one of the rest has his own ship, to thee the one most great ship is intrusted ; the Universal Church herself, made out of all Churches, diffused through the whole world." [1]

[1] S. Bernard, *De Consid.*, lib. ii. c. 8.

SECTION VI.

S. PETER'S PRIMACY AND THE ROYAL SUPRE-MACY.

AND now, what do we, as English Christians, owe to the Chair of Peter? *We owe it everything.* If it is "the root and womb of the Catholic Church" in general, how much more to us in particular!

When Augustine, the Monk, came into England with his band of Missionaries, did he come of himself, or was he *sent?* Who gave him *mission?* Who gave him *spiritual jurisdiction?* Who empowered him to be Primate over England, and to create other Bishops? A power is wanted for all this. Whence did he get it?

Not from the Kentish king, for he was not yet gathered into the fold of Christ himself; how could he *send?*

And had he been a sheep of the fold, how could he give mission to a shepherd?

Nor, again, was he monarch of England. How could he assign all England for a spiritual province?

Augustine derived his mission from S. Peter's Chair.

Augustine derived his power to create other Bishops, and to assign them dioceses, from S. Peter's Chair.

Augustine derived authority over them, when so created, from S. Peter's Chair.

Augustine's successors retained the authority which he had held by commission from S. Peter's Chair.

That English Church arose, parcelling out the island, and irrigating every plot of it with the life-giving water of the Gospel.

The fountain-head was in S. Peter's Chair.

As a living member, it made part of a living Body; and as that Body was ruled and maintained by a head, so was the member.

The head was S. Peter, living also in his successors.

What part had the civil power in all this?

It *allowed* the spiritual power to act; it added to its actions civil authority and privileges; it con-firmed, by the sanction of temporal laws, those assignations of spiritual subjects which the spiritual power had made.

But it never *made* these by and of itself; it never claimed to *send* labourers into the vineyard of the Lord.

It preserved and maintained the civil jurisdiction in these mixed causes when it came into contact with the spiritual; but it never claimed to *originate* this spiritual jurisdiction itself, or to be *supreme judge*, or *judge* at all, in matters of faith.[1]

[1] See this learnedly proved in the late pamphlet of Archdeacon Manning *The Appellate Jurisdiction of the Crown*, etc.

Augustine, the Bishop, had one domain; Ethelbert, the King, had another. He was Augustine's *spiritual child*, and *temporal lord*.

For more than nine hundred years this relationship continued; and as it is founded in first principles of the Christian Faith, the only marvel is, that it can be needful to set it forth, as if it were doubted by any.

But at least the whole ancient Church of England was built on it.

Leaving his days of prayer and peace, S. Augustine went forth from that monastery on the Roman hill, visited and loved by how many English pilgrims, for how many hundred years! He was sent, as yet a priest only, with mission from the Prince of the Apostles, that when the shadow of Peter passed over them, the slaves might become sons, and the Angli Angeli.

These were the words of S. Gregory: "To Augustine your ruler, whom we make your Abbot, be in all things humbly obedient, knowing that whatever you fulfil by his admonition will in all things profit your souls. The Almighty God protect you with His grace, and grant me to see the fruit of your labour *in the eternal country*. Since if I cannot labour with you, I may be found with you in the joy of your reward, for I wish to labour with you. God preserve you safe, most beloved sons." [1]

At the command of S. Gregory, Augustine afterwards receives consecration as Bishop from Virgi-

---

[1] S. Greg., *Ep.*, vi. 51.

lius the Primate of Arles. And this alone would prove how completely distinct is the question of jurisdiction from that of order. Virgilius had no authority whatever to *send* Augustine into England, but at the command of his spiritual superior he could confer upon him those powers which spring from consecration, for the *exercise* of which S. Gregory alone gave him *mission*. To this Bishop Virgilius S. Gregory had before granted " the pall," that is, authority to represent himself over all the Bishops of Gaul. " Because," he says, " it is plain to all *whence* the Holy Faith came forth, in the regions of Gaul, when your Brotherhood asks afresh for the ancient custom of the Apostolic See, what does it, but as a good child, recur to the bosom of its mother?" " And so we grant your Brotherhood to represent ourself in the Churches which are in the kingdom of our most excellent son Childebert, according to ancient custom, which has God for its author." [1]

And so the same power which gave the Bishop of Arles authority over all the Bishops of France, committed England and its future Bishops to Augustine.

Thus, in another letter, S. Gregory empowers Augustine to constitute two provinces, his own, and that of York, each with its Bishops; and he adds to him personally, " Let your Fraternity have all the Bishops of Britain subject to you; by authority of our Lord God." [2]

---

[1] S. Greg., *Ep.*, lib. v. 53.   [2] *Ep.*, lib. xi. 65.

In answer to a question of S. Augustine, he says, in another place: " We give you no authority over the Bishops of Gaul; but we commit to your Fraternity the care of all British Bishops." [1]

Thus the Anglican hierarchy sprung up under S. Gregory's hand : her Primacies were instituted by him, and maintained by him. Every successor of S. Augustine received afresh from every successor of Gregory the continuance of the original mission and jurisdiction.

Thus Boniface V. writes to Justus, the fourth Archbishop, A.D. 622 : " Moreover we send to your Fraternity the pall, *granting also to you to celebrate the ordination of Bishops*, when need requires." [2]

Pope Honorius sends, at the request of King Edwin, palls to the two Archbishops of Canterbury and York, with permission that when one dies the survivor should consecrate another. " He may fill up his place with another Bishop *by this our authority*, which, as well out of regard to your affection as on account of the great space between us, *we are induced to concede*." [3]

The same Pope writes to the Archbishop Honorius, A.D. 626 :

" You ask that the authority of your See should be confirmed by the privilege of our authority. Therefore, according to the old custom which your Church has kept from the times of Augustine, your predecessor, of holy memory, by the authority of blessed Peter, Prince of the Apostles, we grant to

[1] *Ep.*, lib. xi. 64.   [2] Mansi, tom. x. 550.
[3] *Ibid.*, x. 580.

you, Honorius, and to your successors for ever, the Primacy of all the Churches of Britain. Therefore we have ordered all the Churches and regions of England *to be subjected to your jurisdiction*, and in the City of Cánterbury let the Metropolitical place and honour of the Archiepiscopate, and the head of all the Churches of the English people, be kept for the future."[1] And he prays that God would confirm with perpetual stability the Archbishop, "following the rule of your *Master* and *Head*, S. Gregory."

So in the year 657 Pope Vitalian writes to our Archbishop Theodore :

"We learn your desire for the *confirmation* of the diocese subject to you, because in all things you desire to shine by our privilege of Apostolical authority. Wherefore we have thought good at present *to commend to your most wise Holiness all the Churches in the island of Britain*. But now, by the authority of blessed Peter, Prince of the Apostles, to whom power was given by our Lord to bind and to loose in Heaven and in earth, we, however unworthy, holding the place of that same blessed Peter, who bears the keys of the kingdom of Heaven, grant to you, Theodore, and your successors, all that from old time was allowed, for ever to retain unimpaired, in that your Metropolitical See, in the City of Canterbury."[2]

Yet these powers might be withdrawn or changed by him who gave them ; for we find, in the year

---

[1] Mansi, tom. x. 580, 583.   [2] *Ibid.*, tom. xi. 24.

795, Kenulph, King of Mercia, writing to solicit Pope Leo III. to restore to Canterbury that part of its province which his predecessor Hadrian, at the request of King Offa, had erected into an Archiepiscopal province for Lichfield. And this prayer is granted by the Pope. At the same time all the Bishops of England petition the Pope that the favour of one Archbishop consecrating the successor of the other, which had been interrupted by the troubles of the times, might be restored; and that the pall might be granted without going to Rome for it.[1]

At a Council held at Rome in 680, Pope Agatho had ordered that each Archbishop in England, "who for the time is honoured with the pall by this Apostolic See,"[2] may promote and ordain the Bishops subject to him. In the same Council, Wilfred is restored to the See of York.

In the year 1072, a contest arose by reason of Thomas, Archbishop of York, denying the Primacy of Canterbury over his See. A Council was held in Winton, by order of Pope Alexander, to terminate this, and Archbishop Lanfranc communicates to the Pope the result, that clear proof of his Primacy over all England had been adduced. "As the greatest strength and foundation of the whole cause," he says, "there were produced the grants and writings of your predecessors, Gregory, Boniface, Honorius, Vitalian, Sergius, Gregory, and the last Leo, which from time to time,

[1] Mansi, xiii. 960, 989.   [2] *Ibid.*, tom. xi. 180-183.

11

from various causes, were given or transmitted
to the Prelates of the Church of Canterbury and
the Kings of England."[1]

As the Archbishop's Primacy extended over all
England, and comprehended the ordaining of
Bishops and celebrating of Councils, to prove that
it was granted to him and maintained by the
authority of the Pope, is to prove that mission and
jurisdiction to govern the whole Church of England
proceeded perpetually from S. Peter's Chair.

Thus, whoever might nominate and whoever
might elect Bishops, the power which constituted
a particular person to govern a particular diocese
was derived mediately or immediately from the
See of Peter : that is, this See was the perpetual
fountain-head of mission and spiritual jurisdiction.
The Primacies which it had created, it likewise maintained ; and that which was originally a com-
munication of S. Peter's authority (for from him
alone it comes that one Bishop is superior to
another), would subsist throughout by union with
S. Peter.

He who is the source of spiritual jurisdiction is
necessarily the Supreme Judge of doctrine.

But that which the See of Peter was, ages before
the very foundation of the See of Canterbury,
in the whole Church, it seems hardly necessary to
prove, that it was always *in a province of the Church*.
Could any province of the Church determine a
point concerning the faith by and of itself, the

---

[1] Mansi, xx. 23.

least evil to which that must lead would be the dismemberment of that province from the rest of the Body. For what can insure unity of faith without submission to a common head ? This even our Lord did not attempt, even in a body of twelve. How can there possibly exist "one Episcopate, of which a part is held by each without division of the whole," unless there be one law for that whole Episcopate, maintained by one authority within it : as the very Saint who sets forth this idea of the Episcopate observes, " Unity is preserved in the source "?

But, as a matter of fact, for more than nine hundred years the See of S. Peter was in this nation the Supreme Ecclesiastical Judge, and matters of faith could be carried before it, as the court of appeal in last resource.

And, as a matter of fact, for nine hundred and sixty years sixty-nine Archbishops sat in the seat of S. Augustine at Canterbury, by the authority of him who sent S. Augustine.

But by whose authority did the seventieth sit? who gave to Dr. Parker not his orders, not his episcopal character, but *mission*, to execute the powers which belong to that character in the determinate See of Canterbury, and *authority* to execute the powers of a Primate in the province of Canterbury?

To this no answer can be given but one—Queen Elizabeth gave, or at least attempted to give, that mission and that authority.

Let us simply state historical facts.

Queen Elizabeth at her accession found the ancient relation, which for nine hundred and sixty years had subsisted between the See of S. Peter and the Church of England, restored by the act of her sister, after its disturbance by her father and brother. This relation consisted mainly in two points—that the Pope instituted all Bishops, and was the Supreme Ecclesiastical Judge.

Queen Elizabeth caused an Act of Parliament to be passed, depriving the Pope of these two powers. And this Act was passed in spite of the remonstrances of the Episcopate, the Convocation, and the two Universities.

But she did not stop there. Who was to possess these two powers? Somewhere they must be. She coveted them for her Crown: she took and annexed them to that Crown.

She made herself Supreme Ecclesiastical Judge by causing the appeals, which had ever been made from the Court of the Archbishop to the Pope, to be made to the Crown. More need not be said on this head, as all the Courts of the kingdom have just affirmed this power to exist in the Crown; and as her Majesty, in exercise of her authority as Supreme Ecclesiastical Judge, has just reversed the sentence of the Archbishop's Court, and decreed that the Clergy of the Church have it wholly at their option to preach and teach that infants are regenerated by God in Holy Baptism, or that such a doctrine is "a soul-destroying heresy:" nay, as the perfection of liberty, the same clergyman can now at the font, in the words of the Baptismal

Service, declare his belief in the former doctrine, and in the pulpit proceed to enforce the latter!

She took to herself, likewise, the power of *instituting* Bishops, which is of originating mission and jurisdiction; for every Bishop of the Anglican Church has been from that time instituted by order and commission from the Crown, and by that alone. Now it has been well said, that " Sovereigns who covet spiritual authority have never dared to seize it upon the altar with their own hands : they know well that in this there is an absurdity even greater than the sacrilege. Incapable as they are of being *directly* recognised as the source and regulators of religion, they seek to make themselves its masters by the intermediacy of some sacerdotal body enslaved to their wishes : and there, Pontiffs without mission, usurpers of the truth itself ; they dole out to their people the measure of it which they think sufficient to check revolt ; they make of the Blood of Jesus Christ an instrument of moral servitude and of political schemes, until the day when they are taught by terrible catastrophes that the greatest crime which sovereignty can commit against itself and against society is the meddling touch which profanes religion." [1]

Dr. Parker was instituted by four Bishops without a diocese, who had no power whatever of their own to give mission to the See of Canterbury : they professed to act under Queen Elizabeth's commission.

[1] Le Père Lacordaire.

But to show how the fountain of this mission
and spiritual jurisdiction was made to reside in the
Crown, we need only refer to the law which enacted,
that in case an Archbishop should refuse within a
certain time to institute a Bishop at the command
of the Crown—*a case which in three hundred years
has never occurred,* though Dr. Hoadley and Dr.
Hampden have been among the persons instituted—
the Crown might issue a commission to any other
Bishops of the province to institute, thus overruling
the special authority of the Archbishop as Archbishop.

Moreover, the letters patent of every Colonial
Bishop declare in the most express words that
Episcopal jurisdiction to govern such and such a
diocese, which the letters patent erect, is granted
by the Crown.

And not only does the Crown *grant* this jurisdiction, but it can *recall* it after it has been once
granted.

Take the latest exercise of this power.[1]

" The Queen has been pleased, by letters patent
under the great seal of the United Kingdom, to
reconstitute the Bishopric of Quebec, and to direct
that the same shall comprise the district of Quebec,
Three Rivers, and Gaspe *only,* and be called the
Bishopric of Quebec : and Her Majesty has been
pleased to name and appoint the Right Rev. Father
in God, George Jehoshaphat Mountain, Doctor of
Divinity, *heretofore Bishop of Montreal, to be Bishop*

---

[1] *London Gazette.*

of the said See of Quebec. Her Majesty has also been pleased to constitute so much of the ancient diocese of Quebec as comprises the district of Montreal to be a Bishop's See and Diocese, to be called the Bishopric of Montreal, and to name and appoint the Rev. Francis Fulford, Doctor of Divinity, to be ordained and consecrated Bishop of the said See of Montreal." [1]

All that the Archbishop has to do in such a matter is to give Episcopal consecration to a person so designated, on pain of having his goods confiscated, and his person imprisoned : *but he does not give the diocese or the mission.*

Her Majesty likewise—in the exercise of Papal authority—has created sundry Metropolitans, as of Calcutta, to whom she has subjected all India ; and Sydney, to whom she has subjected not only Australia, but Van Diemen's Land and New Zealand.

[1] Since this was written, a judgment of the Privy Council, accepted and ratified by the Crown, in the case of Dr. Colenso, has decided that the grant of spiritual jurisdiction from the Crown to Bishops in colonies which possess a parliamentary constitution is invalid in law. They become, therefore, Bishops without dioceses. It is stated in the papers that Dr. Selwyn and the other Anglican Bishops in New Zealand have in consequence petitioned the Queen to be allowed to return their letters-patent, which professed to give them jurisdiction. The papers do not state whence Dr. Selwyn and his brethren propose to get it for the future. It would seem as if the question of spiritual jurisdiction were not at all considered in the Anglican Church; yet absolution given by a true priest without jurisdiction is invalid; and this fact alone, without going into the question whether her priests are true priests and her Bishops true Bishops, annuls all absolutions in the Church of England.

Now here let me observe two things.

First, that the power to nominate for election, or to elect one to be a Bishop, is quite distinct from the power to institute or confirm, which latter *is the deliverance of · the spiritual power of government.* The former privileges may be and are exercised by the civil power; but the latter authority must be derived from a spiritual source.

Secondly, the civil power may, if it so choose, give the sanction of civil law to the assignations of dioceses made by the spiritual power; and attach a certain *civil* validity to the spiritual acts of Bishops instituted by spiritual power. But here the case is quite different. The diocese is made and erected, divided and altered, solely by the civil power. The spiritual jurisdiction actually possessed by a Bishop over his flock is taken away, as concerns a part of that flock, and conferred upon another. The Bishop is purely passive under this. And so particular Bishops, already supposed to be under the See of Canterbury, are without permission of that See subjected to an intermediate Metropolitan.

Now the whole principle of the Anglican Reformation consists in these two things,—that the civil power is made the origin of Mission and Spiritual Jurisdiction, and the Supreme Ecclesiastical Judge. Those who ask for these things to be altered ask that the Reformation would be pleased to undo all that it did amiss, and so restore itself to Catholic Unity. Would that they may be heard !—but there are few signs of it.

And the whole of what I have written in the preceding five sections shows that the Papal authority consists in exactly these two points. And thus it was that Queen Elizabeth took and transferred the Papal Supremacy to herself. And thus it is that authority to administer the Sacraments of our Lord Jesus Christ in this or that place or district, the keys of the kingdom of Heaven, the power to bind and loose, are pretended to be given by an earthly Sovereign. Can there be found in the history of eighteen hundred years a heresy more directly anti-christian than this ? It strikes at the very heart of the Church of God.

From the beginning the crime of being a creature and a slave of the State has been alleged against the Anglican Establishment. Is this charge true ? and, if so, in what does it consist ?

It is not because a communion is *established* ; because its Bishops are *nominated* by the Crown and sit in Parliament ; because their acts have a civil validity ; because its Clergy are civil officers, —that it can be justly called a creature or a slave of the State. All this may be innocently, may be rightly, may be most happily. But a communion is the creature and the slave of the civil power when the origin of its mission and spiritual jurisdiction, and the supreme judgment upon its doctrine, are vested in the civil power.

But to return to Queen Elizabeth. Armed with this civil law, which extinguished the supreme jurisdiction of S. Peter's See, and its institution of Bishops, and transferred both these powers to the

Crown, imposing an oath for their maintenance, she ordered this oath to be administered to the existing Bishops. The Primacy was vacant, and sixteen members of the Episcopate alone survived. Of these, *fifteen* refused to sever that link between their Sees and the See of Rome, which had subsisted for nine hundred and sixty years, from the very foundation of the Church ; refused beside to acknowledge the transference of the two above-named spiritual powers to the Crown. In virtue of that law they were deposed.

One Bishop, Kitchen of Llandaff, had the heart to accept these conditions, and continued on in his See, surrendering to courtiers the greater part of its endowments.

But even he took no part in the confirmation or consecration of the new Primate.

And so the ancient Episcopate, which derived its succession from S. Augustine, and its mission from S. Peter, became extinct in banishment, in captivity, and in duress. The Episcopate which for well-nigh a thousand years had formed, and civilised, and blessed England in a thousand ways, and by which it was a member of the great Christian Body, was swept away.

And a new Episcopate, deriving its mission from Queen Elizabeth, and perpetually dependent for its jurisdiction on the Crown of England, and owning in that Crown its Supreme Ecclesiastical Judge, arose. This is its origin, this the principle on which it is built, the subjection of the spiritual power to the civil in spiritual things, in faith, and in discipline. *Humanam conati sunt facere Eccle-siam.* They attempted, and they have succeeded. For myself, now that after long years of pain and distress, of thought, of inquiry, and of prayer, since by the mercy of God the light has broken upon me, let me say as much as this,—for not to say it would be to conceal the strongest conviction, neither formed in a hurry, nor reached without great suffer-ing,—let those who can put their trust in such a Church and such an Episcopate, those who can feel their souls safe in such a system, work in it, think for it, write for it, pray for it, and *trust their souls to it.* But the duty which I owe to Almighty God, and the regard which I have for my salvation, compel me to declare my belief, by word and act, that it is an *imposture,* all the more dangerous to the souls of men, to the affectionate, to the obedient, to those who believe that there is "one Body and one Spirit," because it pretends to be a member of the Catholic Body, with which it has broken the essential relation, and to possess spiritual powers which it has indeed forfeited.

SECTION VII.

THE EFFECTS OF S. PETER'S PRIMACY AND OF THE ROYAL SUPREMACY.

THE Primacy which our Lord set up for ever in His Church in the person of S. Peter and his successors was so set up to maintain unity of faith and communion.

That Primacy was finally abolished in the Anglican Establishment by Queen Elizabeth, and two of the chief powers belonging to it attached to her throne, powers which cannot be separated;—that is, to be the Source of Spiritual Jurisdiction, and the Supreme Judge of doctrine. Have the two effects intended by the Primacy of divine institution,— unity of faith and of communion,—followed in the system set up under the Royal Supremacy of human institution?

Has the Anglican Church one faith? Has she communion with the Church Catholic throughout the world?

As to faith, the revelation of our Lord has been of late well divided into three great branches, which indeed are sufficiently indicated by the arrangement of the Apostles' Creed, *viz.*, the doctrine of the

Holy Trinity; the doctrine of the Incarnation; the doctrine of the Church.

It was this latter which was assaulted at the time the Anglican Reformation was set up; and of course to this latter we must mainly look to see the unity of the New Church. Has the Anglican communion any one consistent faith concerning the Catholic Church, and the sacramental system, which is in fact the applying of the Incarnation to the mystical Body of Christ and the souls which belong to it? Who will venture to say that it has, *as a whole?* I speak not of this or that party, Evangelical, Latitudinarian, or High Church, or the Oxford movement, within it; but does the Anglican Church, *as a whole*, deliver to men any belief as to where the Catholic Church at this moment is; whether the Roman is part of it or not; whether the Greek is part of it or not; whether Presbyterianism in Scotland is a branch of it or not; whether it is infallible or not; whether, if General Councils may err, the whole Church may err, and teach falsehood for God's truth? Each individual in the Anglican Church will have his own answer, or none, upon these questions. Yet all repeat: "I believe one Holy Catholic Church." How can they believe what they do not know anything about?

Or again, as to the benefits of Holy Baptism; are not the two great sections of the Establishment at daggers drawn about these—full of misconceptions even as to their own meaning?

Or only conceive that a late trial had turned upon the nature of the Holy Eucharist, instead of Baptism. The mind revolts at the thought of the blasphemies which would have been uttered, and the unbelief in that holy mystery which would have been shown.[1]

Now, not to mention the effects conveyed by Confirmation, and Orders, and Sacramental Absolution, there is not a rural deanery in England whose members could meet together without all or either of the above questions being an apple of discord, if flung among them.

But there is one point which runs right into the heart of him who is charged with the care of souls, and day by day leaves its sting there. The Anglican Church abolished at the Reformation that discipline of penance which existed all over the world. What has she substituted for it? Are her children to sin and sin on, for months and years together, and *restore themselves* when they please to the communion of the Church? sin on, to the very bed of death, in trust upon God's indulgence? Or what living bond of connection is there between the pastor and his flock *in health?* How can he ever come to close quarters with the secret sins of the individual conscience? How to deal with sins

---

[1] Since this was written, a trial respecting the Anglican doctrine of the Eucharist was about to take place; but the maintainer of a sort of Real Presence pleaded that the time limited by the Act for trial had elapsed, and was very glad to escape from a decision by aid of this technical objection. Truly a heroic position for one who fancied that he was asserting a doctrine which is indeed the dearest privilege of the true Church, but which it seems he was content to hold as his individual opinion, denied by as many as list of ministers and laymen in the Anglican Church.

committed after Baptism is a question of the
utmost daily moment to the clergy. How is it
ruled for them in Anglicanism?

They have each to teach souls the way to
Heaven; to teach young children, as well as to
remind adults, of the privileges and duties of
baptised persons; and how to be restored if they
sin. They have all to attend death-beds, and
sinners laden with guilt: are they to hear their
confessions, or tell them to confess to God alone?
to give them absolution, or to instruct them that
God alone forgives sins, and *not* by His ministers?

These several parties will answer these questions
in different ways. In the meantime the sinner
dies !

Do Anglican Bishops authorise auricular confession, or no? or, if they are asked the question,
put it off with an ambiguity?[1]

Is the doctrine of the Apostolical Succession
taught or not by the Anglican Church, or is it "an
open question"? A Bishop lately denied it in
strong terms, preaching on a solemn public occasion
at S. Paul's Cathedral, I think before the great
Missionary power of the Church; the consequence
was, that he was not asked to print his sermon.

Yet one would think this doctrine of some importance to the being of a Church.

Is it not universally felt that the Prayer-book
looks one way, and the Articles another? The
remains of the Catholic spirit in the former consort

---

[1] These are facts which have come to the writer's knowledge.

ill with the flagrant virus of the Reformation in the latter. It is a great contest which is to interpret the other : but the Privy Council seems to have turned the scale in favour of the Articles.

Thus it appears that the whole body of doctrine which was attacked at the Reformation remains in the Anglican system in a state of uttermost confusion. All that it has of good is that which it derived unaltered from the Roman Church : where it attempted to change, it set up nobody knows what, but something so indefinite, so ambiguous, so chameleon-like, in a word, so *dishonest*, that Evangelical and Anglo-Catholic claim it each for themselves. That is, a compromise was made of the whole sacramental system : and a royal decree now comes forth that the clergy may teach contradictories about it.

And is this indeed God's truth ?—did our Lord set up a Church for this, that men might be tossed about with every wind of doctrine? But I go no further in a subject on which one might write a volume. I only wish to show the necessary result of a fatal principle.

And as to unity of communion with the rest of the Church, what has the Royal Supremacy done? —not merely severed it, as a fact, but made it *impossible.*

Other communions are unhappily schismatical, as being *de facto* disjoined from the Head : but they are not built upon, and do not consecrate, the schismatical principle. Greeks or Armenians might once more accept S. Peter's Primacy to-morrow.

The very Monophysites have the hierarchical principle in perfection, and still look up to S. Mark's chair, even in its degradation, as the centre of unity ; and they may one day remember that S. Mark was sent by S. Peter. But Anglicanism is founded on the very principle of denying S. Peter's Primacy, a principle of isolation and severance, which terminates the unity of the Church with each individual Bishop, or rather makes all alike subject, as Bishops, to the civil power. Were this carried out, there would be as many Christianities as there are Christian nations. But enough of divisions which sadden the inmost heart, and lead it to the conclusion that there is no Church upon Earth ; for this every *consistent* Anglican must believe.

Is he not told that the Roman Church, the Greek Church, and the Anglican, which neither teach one creed, nor are united in one government, make up yet one Church ; that is, spiritual bodies, which excommunicate each other, make up that "one Body and one Spirit," which has "one Lord and one Faith"? When the individual conscience asks : What am I to believe *as a matter of divine faith*, on points where these authorities disagree, what answer can be given? Accordingly, the result, to every thinking mind, of Anglicanism is, that there is at present no divine teacher upon Earth at all, whom we are bound to believe and obey. That is *naked infidelity*. Let me entreat those to consider this, who seem to have made up their minds to substitute what they call "loyalty" to the Anglican Church *for maintenance of the*

Catholic Faith, in whose name they once said great things.

Now turn to the other side.

Has the *Divine* Primacy effected the purpose for which it was instituted? Has it maintained unity of faith and of communion?

As to faith, go where you will, and within the bosom of that communion which is built on the rock of S. Peter's Chair, you will find no variance of belief on that threefold cord of doctrine mentioned above. Neither Clergy nor Laity differ as to the doctrine of the Most Holy Trinity, the Incarnation, and the Church, *nor as to all the consequences derived from them.* The Parish Priest pursues his daily task in no doubt as to the instruction of the young, the recovery of the wandering, the consolation of the dying. Councils of Bishops meet in all directions, and send the result of their consultations and prayers to the common Shepherd of all, without contest, without variation of belief, from one end of the earth to the other. The Host comes forth in procession, and every heart is lifted up to the Author of Salvation, every head bowed in worship; one solemn feeling of the Real Presence fills a great church, and inspires its congregation. Moreover, Saints live and grow on it; societies of men and women are inspired by it unto all the labours of self-denying charity.

Take as symbols within the one communion the bare table and the deserted shrine; but comfort, respectability, order, the powers of the world that is.

Within the other, a people hushed in adoration, a cloud of incense, and the Present God ; but poverty, continence, religious communities, the powers of the world to come.

Within the one, among the Clergy themselves, disputes, divisions, indifferences, disbelief of all dogma.

Within the other, a system, acknowledged by all the faithful, encompassing and supporting them from the cradle to the grave.

And as to communion, throughout all regions of the world, how far more justly now than when S. Augustine wrote, may the Catholic say : " I am held in the Catholic Church by the consent of nations and of races, by authority begun in miracles, nurtured in hope, attaining its growth in charity, established in antiquity : I am held by the succession of Bishops down to the present Episcopate from the very See of Peter the Apostle, to whom the Lord, after His resurrection, intrusted His sheep to be fed. Lastly, I am held by the very name of Catholic, which, not without reason, among so many heresies, that Church alone has to such a degree taken possession of, that, though all heretics wish to be called Catholics, yet, if any stranger ask : Where is the Catholic Church? no heretic will dare to show you his own Church."

Would not this seem to be a prophecy uttered fourteen hundred years ago ? and yet as true is what follows :

" Those, therefore, so many and so great most dear bonds of the Christian name with reason hold a believer in the Catholic Church, even if, through the slowness of our natural ability or the demerit of our life, the truth should not as yet have shown itself most fully revealed.   But amongst *you*, where there is none of these things to invite and hold me, *the promise of the truth* alone makes a great noise ; and indeed if this be so plain that it cannot be doubted, it is to be preferred to all those things by which I am held in the Catholic Church : *but if it is only promised and not shown*, no one shall move me from that faith which binds my spirit by folds so many and so strong to the Christian religion."

And now I have given the *Scriptural* authority for S. Peter's Primacy, carried on in his successors ;

Where is the *Scriptural* authority for the Primacy of Queen Victoria ?

I have given the *Patristic* authority, and that of Councils, for S. Peter's Primacy ;

What Fathers and what Councils acknowledge a temporal supremacy of the State over the faith and discipline of the Church ?

Let them be produced ; let us compare the one with the other.

Is there *little* in Holy Scripture for S. Peter's Primacy ?   *How much* is there for the Apostolate and Episcopate itself?   But the words of God are few, only they create and they maintain.   Set the weight of the world on those words which He addressed to Peter, and they will bear it.

But for the Royal Supremacy you have *nothing* to bring from Scripture ; not one word, unless you like, " Render unto Cæsar the things that are Cæsar's, and unto God the things that are God's."

And as for tradition, King Henry and Queen
Elizabeth set themselves against the current of
fifteen hundred years ; they tore up what had
been the root of their own Church for well-nigh
a thousand.   They severed themselves from S.
Peter's See, and they sowed throughout their realm
divisions never-ending,—spiritual severance, isolation, and indifference ; they destroyed that religious
unity which, of all others, is the most precious inheritance of a land.   This they were allowed to
do, and yet at this moment more Bishops, and well-
nigh as many people, subject to S. Peter, own
their temporal sovereignty, as compose that communion which acknowledges their spiritual supremacy, which is itself rent to pieces, and has the
denial even of the doctrine of Baptism imposed on
it by that supremacy.!   It was a fearful vision of
schism and of heresy which the poet saw :

> " A rundlet that hath lost
> In middle or side stave, gapes not so wide
> As one I mark'd, torn from the chin throughout
> Down to the hinder passage, 'twixt the legs
> Dangling his entrails hung, the midriff lay
> Open to view, and wretched ventricle."
>
> —Dante, *Hell*, c. xxviii.

Am I to believe that this hideous phantom is the
teacher sent to me by Almighty God ?   Is this the
dispenser of His Sacraments ? the pillar and ground
of the truth ?

Whither, then, shall I turn, but to thee, O
Glorious Roman Church, to whom God has given,

in its fulness, the double gift of ruling and of teaching?   Thine alone are the keys of Peter, and the
sharp sword of Paul.   On thee alone, with their
blood, have they poured out their whole doctrine.
Too late have I found thee, who shouldst have
fostered my childhood, and set thy gentle and awful
seal on my youth; who shouldst have brought me
up in the serene regions of truth, apart from doubt
and the long agony of uncertain years.   Yet before
I understood thee, I could admire; before I acknowledged thy claims, I could see that undaunted
spirit which would resign everything save the
inheritance of Christ; that superhuman wisdom, by
the gift of which, while "earthly states have had
single conquerors or legislators, a Charlemagne here,
a Philip Auguste there; in Rome alone the spiritual
ruler has dwelt for ages, smiting the waters of the
flood again and again with the mantle of Elijah,
and making himself a path through them on the
dry land."[1]   But now I see that the God of Elijah
is with thee.   O too long sought, and too late found,
yet be it given me to pass under thy protection the
short remains of this troubled life, to wander no
more from the fold, but to find the Chair of the
Chief Shepherd to be indeed "the shadow of a
Great Rock in a weary land"!

[1] *Church of England cleared from Schism*, p. 394.

www.ingramcontent.com/pod-product-compliance
Lightning Source LLC
Chambersburg PA
CBHW030829020726
47499CB00006B/2136